COUNT CAPRIOLI'S
WONDERFUL ADVENTURES AT Sea

PETER FISCHER SORENSON

Ordering Information:

Prime Seven Media
518 Landmann St.
Tomah City, WI 54660

Printed in the United States of America

Grönland
Nord-Amerika
Amsterdam
Paris
Bermudas
Sargasso-See
Azoren
Atlantik
Afrika
Jamaica
West-Indien
Süd-Amerika
Paramaribo
N
W
O
S
Äquator

TABLE OF CONTENTS

If you give luck a chance.....................................1

The ride on a shark.......................................7

Captain Bull's aristocratic barber 17

Larissa appears and Bilg becomes a soldier 23

Witzi the dachshund......................................28

Caprioli becomes uncle Cyps 35

Gold! Gold! Gold! 39

The battle with the giant octopus.....................43

An Adventurous Bear Hunt 51

The Wondrous Throw 56

Strange Friendships 60

Natas Scheitanoff......................................64

A heavy conscience 71

The battle with pirates 74

Surprise on all sides..................................79

The cargo of the "Vlissingen" 87

The Cheese Battle..................................93

Kidnapped to the North Pole 103

The Polar Bear 108

On horseback over the ocean...114

A confused servant and a royal gift 120

The Pirate Treasure and an Unexpected Adventure. ... 128

How the Brigantines were saved and

the Gold Treasure salvaged. 135

To each his own 145

The Seahorses 151

Bilg becomes captain's apprentice and plays ghost....157

Thirst...166

Hope and... 174

Wonderful Rescue 179

The sea snake..186

Super fast travel without wind...195

The greeting in Paramaribo... 203

Big decision are made 211

More intrigue from Scheitanoff 225

Disappeared!... 237

Farewell...246

Near the goal..258

THE CHARACTERS

Cyprian Amadeus Count Caprioli

Secret agent and diplomat for the Austrian Government,
at the moment commander of a fleet of ships belonging
to the Dutch-West India Company – Anno Domini 1715

The Counts companions:

Pelegrin	the count's elderly Hungarian valet
Habakuk	the count's bodyguard
Frank Bull	the captain of the ""Fantoma""
Nieselpriem	the helmsman of the ""Fantoma""
Borromaus	chief gunnery officer, formally pirate
Bilg	cabin boy of the ""Fantoma"" and ...?

The passengers on the ""Fantoma""

Larissa van Groenhagen	daughter of the governor of Dutch Guyana
Baba	her black servant

His Excellency Natas Scheitanoff

Also appearing

Bichler	the Austrian gunnery officer of the "Imago"
Bjoerkr	captain of the "Imago"
Dierk Opzoom	captain of the "Vlissingen" which was sunk by pirates
Dona Escamalota	sister of the cardinal and special guest of the governor
Pieter van Groenhagen	governor of Dutch Guyana – a very rich businessman, uncrowned king of the Dutch West Indies Company, lifelong friend of Caprioli and Larissa's father

The Ships

"Fantoma"	a frigate Caprioli's flag ship
"Imago"	a frigate in Caprioli's fleet
"Hell", "Death" & "Devil"	the pirates brigantines .. Later renamed to Larissa, Bilg & Caprioli

IF YOU GIVE LUCK
A CHANCE

Carefully Bilg opened the door to the harbour side tavern "The Golden Apollo" In Amsterdam. Muffled speech, tobacco smoke and the smell of wine overwhelmed his senses. He had to cough. It took him a while before he could spy the form of Captain Bull. With a glass in his hand, the mighty man was leaning at the end of the bar. He was having a conversation with a short, stubby man who spoke to him waving his hands in the air. This man's face was wrinkled like a dried up prune, with deep set shark like eyes.

And this one, the tall slim one with the hooked nose and silver white goatee? Dressed in his sky blue coat with gold epaulettes, he sat with his long stretched out legs at the table playing dice with Borromaus, the chief gunnery officer. No doubt this was the war commander himself, the mysterious "Count Caprioli"! Bilg had never seen him before, but recognised him immediately from the descriptions he had heard of him.

He slid in behind him and looked over his shoulder. The count ignored the young one.

Bilg carefully touched his arm and whispered in his ear:"Count, a favourable wind has come up and the fleet can sail. The coxswain 'Nieselpriem sent me...!"

The chief gunnery officer just threw a seventeen with his dice, stroked his goatee and collected the 2 gold pieces from the centre of the table. "I won" he said with his from gunpowder roughened voice. His right eye shot a dark look at the count. The left one he always kept shut; from all the aiming it looked like a wrinkled line. With an emotionless face, Count Caprioli gathered the 3 dice and let them drop into the leather cup and turned to Bilg:

"What are you saying cabin boy? The coxswain sent you – A sailing wind has come up? Fantastic! Tell the captain right away, he is standing over there".

Caprioli's eyes swiftly examined the faces around him. He had come to sit with the officers of the ""Fantoma"" in the seaman's tavern to get to know them before the dangerous upcoming trip.

"Do you want to keep playing Count?" asked the chief gunnery officer excitedly "But I am sure that even you won't throw 18!"

Caprioli inclined his head and then looked up.

"How do you know that I can't throw 18..?"

"Because – because you haven't been able to do so until now and because I've never been able to do it"

"So that's your opinion ...?"

Caprioli stood up and weighed the cup in his hand thoughtfully.

The innkeeper, Captain Bull and a few other guests that had secretly followed the game, approached with curiosity. The count took a gold coin from the pile next to him and placed it in the middle of the table.

"Only those that give luck a chance, can achieve the unusual! I bet that I will throw 18. Who will bet?"

"Me Count!" grunted Captain Bull through the jungle of his black beard. Sure of winning he placed a gold coin next to the counts.

Caprioli took the leather cup, shook it and placed it upside down on the table but did not lift it. With a quick movement, he took a second cup from the next table, shook it and placed it upside down on the table next to the first one.

"Well, how many points do I have...?"

"The second cup does not count" growled the Captain "You have to have 18 with the first one"

"The gold coins are already yours Captain" grinned the innkeeper.

Thoughtfully Caprioli lifted the first cup. All three dice showed 6 points.

"Blast – pure chance" Bull angrily stroked his beard.

"Chance and luck take the same path captain!"

Caprioli picked up the second cup and again all three dice showed 6.

The innkeeper's jaw dropped open. He lowered his violet coloured nose almost to the table top to look more closely.

"That's devil's play" grunted Bull.

The right eye in the dark face of the chief gunnery officer flew open:

"You should have been a chief gunnery officer count! I wouldn't be surprised if you were able to shoot down a fly from the top of the mast with a single cannon ball" He said in a raspy voice.

"I don't shoot at flies with cannon balls, my dear friend," said Caprioli with a smile, "but occasionally I can perform other tricks – watch this!"

He picked up one of the gold pieces lying on the table, pushed it against the edge of another one with such skill that it flew in a wide arc directly into the still open mouth of the innkeeper.

"This was not luck, but skill gentlemen," said Caprioli with a smirk. "When the innkeeper manages to close his mouth again, he will have the payment for our bill, and now let's get to our ships!"

The innkeeper fished the gold piece out of his mouth and looked at it shaking his head.

Caprioli had to bend his head to get out the door of the tavern. Captain Bull squeezed his bulk sideways through the door frame. Chief gunnery officer Borromaus followed behind, limping with his wooden leg. He wore wide flowing white linen pants and a loose fitting blue shirt. On his head, he wore a red silk kerchief knotted at the back. He had a curved knife in his pearl studded belt on one side and Arabic pistol on the other. In his younger years, he was a feared pirate in the Caribbean. In a sea battle where he lost his right leg to the knee, he was taken prisoner and condemned to death. His incredible marksmanship won him a reprieve. Since then he has loyally served the gentlemen of the Dutch West Indies Company as a chief gunnery officer, feared by all pirates. In memory of his wild youth, he wears his pirate outfit, which his superiors allow as a reward for prowess and loyalty.

THE RIDE ON A SHARK

The ""Fantoma"" made its passage through the dark green waves of the Atlantic Ocean. Her full sails were blindingly white in the sun. The flagship had four fast well armed frigates in her wake. The ships were sent by the Dutch – West Indies Company to deliver five hundred soldiers to Paramaribo in Dutch Guyana. The troops were to relieve the soldiers in the fort. The soldiers were distributed among the five ships.

The commander of this little war flotilla was Cyprian Amadeus Count Caprioli.

The count, standing at the bow of his ship, watched an albatross circling the ship with barely a movement of its giant wings. His huge black personal servant "Habakuk, stood behind him with crossed arms. With his red wide pants, blue jacket with gold embroidery and the expertly turned turban, he gave the impression that he came from a fairy tale world.

Leaning against the foremast, Pelegrin, the count's old valet, was having a discussion with Borromaus the chief gunnery officer.

"With six dice he managed to get 36 points," said Borromaus. "If I hadn't seen it with my own eyes....!"

"When you are near the count you will have to get out of the habit of being surprised dear Sir" Pelegrin told him thoughtfully. His speech still had the melodious sound of his Hungarian background.

"I am not a Sir, but a Senor, as I am originally from "Cartagena" in the Caribbean Sea! Do you know this Spanish fort maybe?" Borromaus replied proudly.

Pelegrin shook his head and slowly continued "Those who spend time with my master find out that reality changes to a dream and a dream becomes reality. The count is wonderful senor. I am telling you in advance, you will never forget this journey!"

"I'll stick with my cannons, they are reality and do not dream", Borromaus replied.

Pelegrin smiled quietly.

"Even with your cannons you could experience unusual things when the count is on board. I could tell you some stories....!

The loud cry of a sailor brought the gunnery officer to the rail. Pelegrin followed him slowly. Caprioli and Habakuk also came along.

In long green foaming mountains, the waves crashed and seemed to be boiling. Hundreds of dolphins played around the ship, chasing each other and leaping high out of the water.

Sailors and soldiers excitedly threw lines baited with chunks of meat, in the hope of catching some of these beautiful mammals. The men had to hold on as the continuously increasing wind and waves made the ""Fantoma"" bounce around like a wild seahorse.

One wave higher than all the others raced towards the ship, and as it broke plucked the count and Habakuk off the deck as if they were just flies.

Pelegrin only received a generous dousing and could still see his master being swallowed by a wave after a strangled cry.

The gunnery officer's vision was temporarily darkened; the wave had deposited the count's three cornered hat on his head. He ripped it off, saw Caprioli emerge from a wave and shouted hoarsely "Count, your hat...!" He threw the hat in a wide arc at the count and grinned with pleasure when he saw that the count had caught the hat and pushed it on his wig. However, immediately he regained his senses and hit himself on the forehead, "Madonna, I threw him the hat – am I crazy?" he stuttered to himself confused.

Pelegrin was dumbfounded from fright, then, heard himself say "Mann overboard! Maan uber Boord....!

Captain Bull also saw the accident from the bridge. Like a wild bull, he gave the command to put a boat over the side, turned the ""Fantoma"" and signalled the rest of the fleet about what happened.

Pelegrin thought that his master and servant were lost forever. The little boat could barely make headway through the towering waves and the flagship could only turn in a wide arc because of the pressure of the wind.

In despair, he took the spyglass which he always had to carry for the Count and searched the waves. There, he discovered him but couldn't believe his eyes. He took the spyglass from his eye, cleaned it with a corner of his coat and leaning far forward on bent knees, once more looked into the waves.

"Oh, tejo isten!" – "Oh my God!" he cried. Caprioli was in the middle of the school of dolphins and to save himself did the next best thing. With a powerful kick, he swung himself onto the back of the nearest animal. Pelegrin saw him riding on one of the huge dolphins. He laughed and waved to the ships as he rode past at high speed. Habakuk followed his example and raced along next to him on another dolphin. His black face was almost grey with seasickness from the unusual motion of his mount. For quite some time, the school of dolphins swam alongside the ships. Suddenly there was unrest in the school. As if by command, the school turned away from the ships and the silver black arrows, shot off to a common goal.

While Caprioli was thinking how to get back to the ships, he saw the reason why the school had suddenly changed direction. A huge shark along with a smaller one, probably his mate, had been attracted by the smell of the meat the sailors had attached to their fishing lines. Because of their greed they ended up in the middle of their worst enemy. The mighty triangular fins ploughed through the water at terrific speed, but the dolphins were quicker; with fantastic force and speed they rammed the sharks with their snouts. They did not bite, because that lesson had been learned by experience, the incredible toughness of shark skin was impossible to penetrate.

Meanwhile, Caprioli also became seasick, and a wish for a calmer ride became stronger and stronger. Suddenly he saw the larger of the sharks speed directly toward him. He let him come quite close, made half a handstand with his right hand held on to his hat with the left and elegantly swung himself on the new mount. This large shark didn't seem to notice the extra weight of the count; he only had eyes for the dolphins. These intelligent mammals avoided the legs of the count while ramming the shark; however, he had no inclination to participate in this battle any longer than he absolutely had to. He took the long gold chain with his medal from his neck and the moment the shark rolled sideways to snap at a dolphin, he swung the chain into its gaping jaw and adjusted it like a horses bridle. Frightened, the monster wanted to dive, but Caprioli jerked up with such force, that like it or not it had to stay at the top. He practised a few manoeuvres he had learned in the riding academy and soon the shark realised that he had to obey. Habakuk followed his master's example and rode along beside him on the smaller shark. He steered his mount with his belt, having wedged the two parts of its buckle in the corners of its jaw. He was happy to have smoother ride under him, wiped the salt water from his face and grinned from ear to ear about the fantastic mount he now had. Now the Count dug in his spurs, waved to Habakuk to follow him and like brides of the wind, the giant fish shot through the waves towards the fleet. Their speed was so great that the bow waves rose like mountains on either side of them. The dolphins temporarily confused, stopped their attack on the sharks. But now they understood. With giant leaps in the air, they pushed and herded the sharks in exactly the direction the count wanted.

The captains of the fleet watched the approach of the Count and Habakuk with their spyglasses. The sailors and soldiers stood by the railings and looked speechless at the spectacle.

Caprioli steered his shark towards the stern of the last frigate, made a slight turn to pass along side the entire fleet. A loud trumpet sounded over the squadron – as if they were all attached to one string – a jolt went through the many gaping sailors and soldiers. They all came to attention and ripped their hats and caps from their heads and held them with outstretched arms to their sides.

In reply, Caprioli removed his three cornered hat and waved back. Riding on his shark in the middle of the ocean he held parade.

Proudly Habakuk followed behind him. Arriving near the flagship the count tightened his hold on the chain and looked for a likely spot along the hull of his ship. Then he lowered his hat in a formal salute. As Caprioli passed the ship the whole company went berserk throwing hats in the air and behaving like crazy people. Luckily no one thought of firing off the cannons or it would have panicked the sharks. Captain Bull stood with spread legs on the bridge. Caprioli yelled out to him to lower a rope ladder. As soon as that was done, the Count, who had passed the flagship by now, guided his mount back to the ship. As he came close to the ladder, he ripped his gold chain out of the jaws of the shark, took hold of the ladder and swung himself over.

Habakuk copied him.

With thunderous applause, and cries of happiness the two of them were welcomed aboard. Habakuk however, did not give them much time. With his enormous bulk, he made a pathway through the crowd to their cabin as they were both soaking wet and cold. With shaking knees from all the excitement, Pelegrin followed them. He could barely stammer a word, but Caprioli understood him even without words.

Captain Bull with clenched lips watched in awe from the bridge holding the railing in his fist like a vice.

The fishing lines with the bait were still hanging in the water. The sharks suddenly released from their captors, got the scent again. None of the dolphins had taken the bait, but these voracious predators couldn't resist. They devoured the bait and were caught. The sailors and soldiers were jubilant – after all, a juicy shark steak was nothing to complain about.

Borromaus leaned against the post leading up to the bridge.

Captain Bull and helmsman Nieselpriem were climbing down on deck, when the gunnery officer heard the captain growl:

"What does such a sophisticated land lubber understand about real seamanship; the deck of a ship in these conditions isn't a promenade after all, it's a shame that the baptism didn't last a bit longer!"

Nieselpriem spat a mouthful of chewing tobacco in a wide arc over the rail and said:

"He does seem to understand a lot about dolphins and sharks though; I would have been eaten by them or at the very least would have drowned!"

"Boulder dash" answered Bull angrily, "with him, it's all luck and chance, nothing else"

The helmsman stuffed another wad of tobacco in his cheek.

"That's exactly it: everyone is lucky once and chance is cheap. He, however, makes luck out of chance and grabs the luck full on. I would love to see you ride on a shark captain!"

Borromaus added:

"I also think that the count did better in the water than you captain on top of the water. You must have learned the turning manoeuvre to pick up the count from a ships boy. Or maybe not...?"

Bull cursed, but did not dare to criticise the gunnery officer. The look in his eye was like a naked dagger.

Nieselpriem turned away smiling.

CAPTAIN BULL'S ARISTOCRATIC BARBER

With long legs crossed, Caprioli sat relaxed in his cabin. Smiling, he stroked his silver white beard. Across from him, Captain Bull sat uneasily in his chair.

"You saw a ghost captain…? Asked Caprioli. His eyes shot blue lightning bolts of mirth at him. The hairy mountain of muscle and meat in front of him twitched. Bull raised his arms threateningly.

"Don't mention his name Count, otherwise we will have more bad luck as can be expected anyway.

"Where did you see him?" Caprioli asked.

"A few minutes ago I saw him sitting on the railing, and the spray that came on board went right through him as if he wasn't there at all!"

Caprioli touched a finger to his chin and turned his head thoughtfully.

"And how do you know that it was a ghost captain? Did you already meet him once?"

Bull looked up surprised and nervous. "Meet him…? God forbid! One just knows and feels…!

Caprioli pouted his lips.

"You feel as much as a millstone which should have been hung around your neck a long time ago. But maybe the similarity between the ghost and another person frightened you?"

Bull blew up his cheeks uncomfortably.

"With which other person…?"

"Well I am thinking about a short little man that you had a secret conversation with on the night prior to our departure in that tavern in Amsterdam. He then disappeared without a trace"

Cold sweat formed on the captain's forehead.

"Do you know this man count? Who is he…? That was the first time I ever saw him."

Caprioli had a mysterious smile on his face, stood up, looked out the window for a few moments and abruptly turned away.

"How much did he give you to smuggle him on board and how much did he promise you to murder me secretly…?"

Caprioli's voice hit Bull's ears like the cracking of a whip. He raised his hands in defence.

"When Habakuk and I were swept into the sea, you stood at the helm captain. At the right moment, you turned the ship in such a way that the breakers had to hit the side of the ship. Then you ordered the most untrained crew to take the worst boat to go after us and then… Bull any sailor could have done better with the manoeuvres. I would have put you in irons a long time ago if I didn't know whom you upset with your greed. So how much gold did you get?"

Bull pushed himself out of the chair with glassy eyes.

Like a crazy man, he groaned:"gold – gold….!"

He ran out of the cabin with roaring laughter.

Habakuk, who until now had stood with crossed arms behind his master, closed the door.

"I think now I have earned a pipe full of tobacco, don't you agree Habakuk?" asked Caprioli. "We will have a few more experiences on this journey with the captain and his ghost."

Habakuk grinned, passed the long Dutch clay pipe to the count and lit it for him.

"Captn is afraid of ghost" he answered with a mischievous look in his shiny eyes, "and the ghost is afraid of you sar"

A big cloud of smoke came out of Caprioli's mouth. He lent back to let himself fully enjoy the taste of his pipe, but the noise of many running feet on deck diverted his attention.

"Habakuk, go have a look what is going on up there" he ordered his servant. Habakuk disappeared. A few moments later one could hear a shrill whistle, which was the secret signal between the count and his servant. Caprioli jumped up, picked up his sabre and rushed out of the cabin.

"My pistols, Pelegrin" he yelled out over his shoulder.

On deck he saw the incredibly strong Habakuk with balled fists, standing opposite a group of sailors and soldiers. One of the sailors had a wetted heavy rope end in his hand and was about to hit Bilg the cabin boy, who was tied down on a low bench.

"Untie him…!" ordered Caprioli.

Habakuk lent down to untie the ropes. Bilg didn't move. Only his balled fists and white knuckles showed that there was still life in him.

Captain Bull watched all this from the bridge. Now he came down the stairs and yelled at the count:"who is in charge of the ships company here? Go to hell and look after your own affairs!"

He ripped the rope end out of the sailors hand, lifted it over his head and wanted to hit Bilg's back. At the same instant Caprioli's sword whistled through the air, and the rope end flew over the railing in a wide arc. Bull only had a tiny bit of rope left in his hand. He stared at it in wonder.

"You are in charge of the ships company, but you are not the master over life and death. The first hit would have made the boy into a cripple and second one could have killed him!"

Caprioli's voice was low, but it carried a warning that sent shivers down the backs of every one.

Bull slowly lifted his head and stared at Caprioli with blood shot eyes. Quickly, he grabbed a boarding axe and went for Caprioli in a crouch.

Habakuk wanted to grab him but one look from the count stopped him. As if he were in a tournament the count slowly took the point of his sabre with his left hand and bent it. Now the captain was upon him and raised the heavy weapon. The sabre flashed like lightning through the air towards the captain's head, three, four times – and the wind blew Bulls head hair and beard over the railing. The captain stared after his flying hair, dropped the axe, and touched the places where only moments ago grew his thick black jungle. With aloud snort he yelled "you will pay for this!" and rushed off.

With a laugh Caprioli yelled after him:" You will be paying as it was I who was your barber!"

As funny as the shaved captain looked, there was only some quiet snickering from the sailors, only the soldiers roared with laughter. With hands in their pockets and bent heads the sailors slid away. Their only hope to escape the wrath of the captain was this strange count.

Meanwhile Habakuk had untied Bilg and helped him to his feet. Crying, Bilg fell on his knees in front of Caprioli. Then he fell unconscious on his side.

Habakuk picked him up in his arms, carried him to the count's cabin and lowered him on a couch.

As Caprioli stroked his blond head he asked:"What did you do young man…?" He opened his eyes for a moment and whispered:"I secretly listened to the captain, he is crazy, and he also smuggled someone on board…."

With a sigh the boys head dropped back on the pillow.

LARISSA APPEARS AND BILG BECOMES A SOLDIER

Somewhere along the wall one could hear a distinct knock, once, twice ….

Pelegrin was writing in his diary. He lifted his head and listened.

Habakuk, who normally has no fear, had a glassy look in his eyes.

"Ghost…!" He almost lost his voice from fright.

"Maybe the ghost wants to visit us" Caprioli said with a mocking voice.

Again there was a knock, lauder and more urgent.

"Well come in then for crying out loud" called Caprioli, not really expecting anyone.

With a soft click, a hidden door opened and a very young lady slid in.

"Shush", don't be frightened !" she whispered with a charming smile, "I saw everything that happened on deck, I just wanted to check on Bilg."

"Ah, the mysterious lady from the bridge is visiting secretly!" Caprioli said and winked at Habakuk to remove the pistols from the table.

"I will explain everything later count Caprioli", answered the young lady, "at the moment the poor cabin boy is the only thing important."

"Let him sleep young lady, have a seat and explain to me why you have been hiding till now and what the meaning of this secret door is."

Caprioli pointed at a chair in invitation.

The young lady sat at the end of the bench where Bilg was lying.

While she replied, Caprioli admired her black locks, the huge eyes which had a gold shimmer, the finely sculptured nose and pearly white skin.

"Just call me Larissa count", she said in a soft voice not to waken Bilg. "The directors of the company in Amsterdam, many of which are good friends of my family, offered the closed aft section of the ""Fantoma"" to me and my black servant. You did know, after all, that you had two passengers on board. I want to visit some relatives in Paramaribo and so that I could come to you for protection at any time, the door was put in, back in Amsterdam. One can also open the door from here; you just have to press on that brass button there. And why I only came know? I wanted to look after Bilg, and so you wouldn't put me ashore, I waited till we passed the last port. You are well known – even the business men in Amsterdam were not too sure about you in this case.

Caprioli squinted and started to play with his medal:"After all the ""Fantoma"" is a ship of war and not really the right place for a young lady. However, I am a gentleman. But tell me: did you live in Amsterdam, Mademoiselle Larissa....?

"No, I spent a year in Paris where I went to school. Why do you ask?"

"Because I would like to know how you found out that I would be taking these troops to Paramaribo!"

"The gentlemen in Amsterdam knew about it!"

"But you were in Paris. I only arrived in Amsterdam two days before our departure and prior to that had no intention of travelling to Paramaribo." Caprioli said with a smile on his face.

"It just happened that way count Caprioli!" she said with an impish look

"Do you know what a half truth is Mademoiselle Larissa...?"

The young lady laughed out loud.

"Naturally I know that: it's a lie! But please be satisfied with what you know now. Maybe I will be able to tell you more soon.

Bilg had woken up and listened with big eyes. Larissa saw this and reached for the young man's hand. "Be happy again Bilg, all ended up well after all!"

"He will beat me to death if he sees me!"

Bilg was still shaking.

"He will do nothing to you my boy!" C0aprioli took a large silver coin from his waist coat and threw it to Bilg.

"There, you will return this coin to the captain on my orders. It is the money that you received from him, when he hired you as cabin boy. And now I will take you in my service, as drummer boy for now. Would you like that....?"

"Count...!"

Bilg jumped up full of joy.

"Its ok Bilg" replied Caprioli,"here is another coin as your hire money; you are a soldier now!"

Caprioli threw him a gold coin. Bilg caught it and didn't know how to thank him.

"Wonderful!" cried Larissa and clapped her hands with happiness. Then she thought for a moment, placed a hand on Bilg's arm who was still shaking and said to Caprioli:

"I have a wish, which I am sure you won't deny me. I have heard so much about your fantastic adventures; please tell us about one, but a happy one! Will you….?"

Caprioli quickly looked at Bilg with a concerned expression.

"Well, Mademoiselle Larissa, I will tell you a funny and happy story"

He crossed his legs comfortably and while Habakuk poured some sweet wine into small glasses he started:

WITZI THE DACHSHUND

"When I was a young man I once owned a female dachshund, her name was Trixi. She was in every way an unusual dog. Against all rules, I loved to take her duck hunting, because she swam like an otter and brought back the birds full of enthusiasm. However she was usually too late: a beautiful duck would sink in deep unreachable water like a rock, or an injured duck would crawl into the reeds or undergrowth, where even Trixi couldn't find it any more.

One day, as she crawled out of the water, again without a duck and looked at me for forgiveness with her doleful eyes, I said to myself "If you could only fly....!" It should have been a consolation for her, but these well meant words stayed in her mind. Because she loved me above all she took these words as a reproach.

We kept a large herd of geese at one of the farms attached to the castle. When in the fall the wild geese migrated north, they always stopped in with the domestic ones to share some of their food. One day I noticed a beautiful large wild gander waddling behind my Trixi. At first Trixi was a bit annoyed by the insistence of the gander, but after a while took it as a compliment. When the wild geese continued on their journey, the large gander stayed behind and they became inseparable. Even with me he lost all his shyness and even accompanied us on the hunt occasionally. One morning Trixi and her gander companion disappeared. It took almost eight days before they showed up again – but they weren't alone any more: a small female dachshund waddled on her short legs between them. I looked at the animal a bit closer and almost died from fright. It was a lovely young dachshund of course, but from his shoulders grew a set of fully developed wings of a wild goose and the down became intermingled with her red brown fur. Full of pride about this strange creature, Trixi snuggled up to me. As she couldn't fly herself, she brought me as a present, a hunting dog with wings. The gander also gave me to understand that some praise was due to him. I managed to hide the incredible pair in an abandoned forest cabin belonging to my father. The little winged dachshund I named "Witzi" because I could not think of a name that suited her better.

Sadly, my old forester Hadrian took Witzi as the devils roast and he kept this opinion even to the time when Witzi was grown up and became a fantastic hunting partner. Witzi had learned to fly and luckily got out of the habit of squawking like a goose. After a short take off run on her little bent legs, she opened her wings and took off like a shot. She circled the cabin and barked happily when she saw Hadrian and me standing by the front door. With his pipe between his teeth, the old forester looked up and disappeared shaking his fists, when I motioned Witzi to come down.

One day my school friend Pieter van Groenhagen came for a visit to come hunting with me and I introduced him to Witzi.

He stared with wide eyes at the winged dachshund and then at me. He was dumbfounded. I however bent down to pick up a small stone, whistled and threw the pebble high in the air. Retrieving was Witzi favourite pastime. She barked once, shot after the pebble as if fired from a pistol, caught it, returned in a wide arc to lay it at my feet and jumped up at me barking happily, waging her little tail.

I gave her a lump of sugar as reward.

My friend Pieter had nerves of steel, but when he saw Witzi's flying demonstration he was beyond himself for a few minutes. Finally he turned towards me again, looked at me with indescribable eyes, threw his rifle over his shoulder and just said: "Well are we going….!"

Along the way he grunted:

"One should try to create a new breed with this funny animal"

I could have come up with this idea myself! I pretended that I had thought of the breeding idea a long time ago and answered:

"That would be difficult, as only this one female exists and if Trixi and the gander…."

"Anyway, one should think about this idea" he rambled on. It was obvious that he wasn't happy about Witzi. As a professional breeder of hunting dogs, he felt slighted by me.

I have never been able to teach Witzi the proper way to hunt. For example, if I shot at a pheasant sitting on a high branch, she thought that I wanted her to retrieve the bullet. With incredible speed she shot after the bullet, caught it with her mouth, stuffed it behind her molars like a piece of chewing tobacco and only then cruised after the pheasant to grab him by the neck. She placed the pheasant at my feet, spat out the bullet and looked up at me with shining eyes waiting for the deserved reward.

Witzi never brought an animal back alive. Whether it was a pheasant, a grouse, a wild duck or a heron – none of them survived the fright of being chased high in the air, by a barking and flying dachshund.

Pieter slowly seemed to have got used to Witzi. However I became a bit suspicious of him when I surprised him and Hadrian the forester, talking about my dogs in the evening.

One day near the end of autumn I lost Witzi forever .She must have had more goose in her little dachshund heart than I realised. A school of grey geese flew over one day, Witzi looked up from her breakfast, listened, happily wagged her tail and shot out through the window like lightening to follow the geese.

Concerned, Pieter, Hadrian and I watched her fly away.

First she caused terrible confusion among the wedge of geese. However when she moved up to the point with her encouraging yapping, the geese reformed their well practised wedge and happily followed her.

"She will never come back" concluded my friend dryly, "she has no character!"

"well excuse me Pieter" I protested

"she doesn't have any" he insisted.

"OK she doesn't have any character" I answered angrily, "but your grandiose idea of breeding flying dachshunds is also finished now!"

"So, you think so…!"

An alarming undertone could be heard in his voice. Forester Hadrian got up and shortly returned with a basket full of eggs, which he held under my nose.

There were about 20 neatly arranged eggs, as large as goose eggs but all with a lovely red-brown colour.

A foreboding thought came to my mind. My heart started beating faster and I looked at Pieter.

"You didn't by any chance…?"

He gave off a short gleeful laugh.

"Of course I did, it was the simplest way. Everything that has wings lays eggs! I taught your little Witzi to lay eggs. But now that she should be sitting on the eggs, this characterless beast takes off."

I went pale with envy as this breeding success left mine in the dark.

"So, how did you manage to do this Pieter?" I asked him stunned and a bit sheepish.

In my imagination I could see swarms of flying dachshunds chasing every flying game bird.

"My secret!" he dryly answered my question.

Then I had an idea.

"Maybe we can find a breeding chicken or goose and slide the eggs under her" I said guilefully. "But do you really think that little ones will come out of these eggs, even though Witzi laid them without having a husband?"

"Why not" answered Pieter surprised. "After all, so many unusual things have happened already!"

I had to accept defeat.

We managed to find a breeding goose who also accepted the eggs.

"Well my dear ones" Caprioli ended his story. "This was the only time in my life that my friend Pieter got the better of me. But nature herself gave me back my honour soon after".

Bilg had listened with open mouth, but Larissa was shaking with laughter.

"How did nature do that, and what happened to the eggs?" she wanted to know.

Well, they did hatch alright, some were deaf, but the rest developed into beautiful geese."

"Geese?" wondered Larissa.

"Yes, but they had to end up in the oven fairly quickly. They...barked. Nobody could stand that!"

Larissa shrieked with laughter.

Bilg looked at the count with big eyes and thought about the story.

CAPRIOLI BECOMES UNCLE CYPS

Larissa was still snorting and laughing into her tiny little handkerchief. It was obvious that it wasn't only the story of the winged dachshund that amused her that much; she must have had another thought in her mind which brought on the constant fits of laughter. Caprioli asked her, but Larissa just shook her head.

Bilg had finally come to his senses, enough, so that the count could send him to Borromaus who equipped him with the uniform of a drummer boy.

Bilg left with sparkling eyes.

Count Caprioli had been to a secret diplomatic mission in Antwerp. During a formal dinner, Mijnheer van Akker

one of the biggest businessmen of the company in Amsterdam, started a conversation with him. This businessman surprised the count, as experienced in matters of war he was, with the offer to lead the relief army of the Dutch-West Indies Company to Paramaribo. Although, Caprioli had finished his affairs and adventures always attracted him, he was not really all that interested in accepting this honourable offer. The ships used for these troop transports were generally old and made this trip of several weeks at see a torturous undertaking.

Mijnheer van Akker however explained to him that this little fleet was made up of battle ready ships and that the famous ""Fantoma"" was to be the flagship. No ship, ploughing the waves of the Atlantic in 1715 was a match for this 3 masted heavily armed vessel. Now Caprioli could not resist any longer, especially because he had wanted to visit the governor of Dutch Guyana the uncrowned king of the Dutch-West Indies Company for a long time. This man was none other than his old school friend and hunting partner Pieter van Groenhagen.

Caprioli almost declined the command after stepping aboard the ""Fantoma"" in Amsterdam. Some of the cabins of the frigate had been rebuilt and luxuriously furnished. The passengers were to be a mysterious and very spoilt young lady and her black servant. This young lady wanted to undertake the dangerous sea voyage to Paramaribo under the protection of Caprioli, but did not wish to meet the count at this stage. In the end the wonderful ship and the possibility of seeing his friend Pieter again convinced him to take the command.

"Did you have other adventures like the flying dachshund and do you ride sharks often when you fall into the water, uncle Cyps?" asked Larissa and interrupted his thoughts.

Caprioli raised his eye brows: "what did you call me....?"

Larissa, frightened, put her hand over her mouth "Oh dear, I let it slip out – can you forgive me uncle Cyps?"

Her nose wrinkled from holding back her laughter and exuberance.

"Uncle Cyps...? repeated Caprioli thoughtfully and seemed to be listening to a far away sound, "that was many many years ago"

It was almost exactly ten years ago, when I called you that in Amsterdam uncle Cyps – I was five years old then. Look at me properly"

"You are not...?"

"Of course uncle Cyps, that's exactly who I am: Larissa van Groenhagen, your God child. Now you know why I particularly wanted to come with you and on this ship. Didn't uncle Hein organise that well to give you the command?"

Caprioli jumped up. He was still doubtful.

"Uncle Hein, your father's brother...?"

"Yes he wanted to get me to Paramaribo safely and you are to be the big surprise for my father".

"But how did you get from Paris to Amsterdam so quickly?"

"It wasn't all that quick uncle Cyps, I had plenty of time. While you had to travel to Rome in spring, an informer of uncle Hein in Vienna found out that your next assignment would probably take you to Antwerp. A servant girl had secretly listened – not without reward of course. The merchants of the company have to have ears everywhere after all. It wasn't very difficult then, to entice the members of the Viennese court to ensure this trip came to reality".

"Wow!" said Caprioli, "so that's how it was! It seems that I was really taken in by uncle Hein. But I am quite happy about this after all" he added grinning. "And what do I get now for consolation..?"

Caprioli opened his arms, but Larissa had to get a chair to stand on to be able to give her tall godfather a consolation and welcome kiss.

GOLD! GOLD! GOLD!

Bilg strutted around in his new colourful uniform, but he had little time to admire himself. The old chief trumpeter Jacob had to teach him how to use the drum sticks correctly and how to master the playing of the general march on the veal skin.

Captain Bull growled; for days now he didn't leave his cabin. Since then coxswain Nieselpriem had the command of the ""Fantoma"". Count Caprioli made no comment about this change, as he knew that Nieselpriem was an excellent seaman and also had his captain's licence for ocean voyages like this one. Also he did not want to make things worse with the already badly hurt pride of Bull.

In the meanwhile the ships company was whispering and giggling. One of the sailors had to try and fix Bulls hair and beard because Caprioli did not do the job with his sword to the satisfaction of the captain. The scuttle-bud around the ship was that he looked so bad that even the ship's ghost was frightened.

One morning Bilg slipped into Caprioli's cabin and announced excited:

"The captain is getting crazier every day, I saw it through the key hole!"

"Through the *keyhole*...?" Caprioli asked with a frown.

"Yes certainly count, he constantly screamed and groaned, so I had a look through the keyhole!"

"And what did you see...?"

He stood in front of a table, rummaged in a pile I could not see and cried and groaned 'gold, gold' but he doesn't have any gold."

Caprioli looked up at Pelegrin, stood up and winked at Habakuk.

"Well I think we should have a closer look at Bull" he said thoughtfully, "I really don't need crazy captains."

Caprioli twisted the door knob of the captain's cabin; it wasn't locked.

As Bilg had reported, Bull stood by a table, rummaged through the invisible pile with greedy hands and threw fistfuls in the air pretending to be showered by the invisible gold. His forehead was moist with sweat and his eyes had a feverish shine. His hair and beard looked like the rats had had a feast.

At the sound of his cabin door opening, Bull stopped his mysterious game and starred at the intruders with an absent minded look. Then with a raspy gargling voice:

"gold! gold! I am filthy rich! I can buy myself a ship, a whole fleet....!"

With his hairy hands he rummaged around the table top as if there really was a mountain of gold before him.

Pelegrin looked at the count with a worried look.

Caprioli said quietly:"It seems that a good old acquaintance is at work here. If that's the case then maybe we can turn this figment of the imagination into earthly reality."

The captain threw another handful of the invisible gold in the air and snorted with contentment. Caprioli quickly stepped up to the table, waved his hand in the air as if catching a fly...In the palm of his hand there appeared a gold coin.

At the same instant, a shower of gold coins came jingling, bouncing and spinning down on the captain's head and shoulders and formed a glistening heap on the table.

From somewhere deep inside the ship came jeering laughter. A frightened scream escaped Habakuk's' lips.

"That was the invisible passenger" whispered Bilg.

"Yes I know our old acquaintance!" Caprioli put a hand on his shoulder.

Bull stood as if frozen, wiped his brow with the back of his hand and appeared to be slowly waking up from a terrible nightmare into a dreamlike reality. Suddenly he threw himself with outstretched arms over the pile of gold and cried:"This is my gold! My gold, gold for me alone!"

He straightened out, looked at the count and his companions with bloodshot eyes, grabbed a chair and held it threateningly above his head.

"Let's go" said Caprioli, and to the captain. "Should you have something to say to me, then you know where to find me."

THE BATTLE WITH THE GIANT OCTOPUS

Caprioli, Larissa and the old and wise valet Pelegrin sat together chatting in the stateroom. Habakuk moved the large fan near the ceiling with evenly and relaxed movements, because in this early hour of the morning the heat was already becoming oppressive.

A scraping noise on the hull made every one stop and listen. It sounded as if the side of the ship scraped against something sandy. An unusual motion went through the frigate and then everything was back to normal.

"What could that have been..? Pelegrin asked. The tip of his nose had gone pale.

"Odd – there are no reefs or sandbars in this region"

"Maybe a whale" whispered Larissa.

There are no whales in this area either, but maybe the ship brushed against another large animal that was asleep under water" Caprioli said thoughtfully. "Here near the Sargasso Sea, the ocean still has many secrets."

"Those who travel with the count must get used to unbelievable monsters – it often appears that the devil himself sends them." said Pelegrin to Larissa. It wasn't sure whether he was just worried or wanted to express a hidden reproach. Caprioli swayed his head. "One should not paint either the devil or monsters on the wall – for the time being a creature of our fantasy is no more than an image of an unknown reality."

A hefty impact went through the ship. The ""Fantoma"" leant dangerously to leeward. "It seems that the devil is trying to find entertainment for us!"

He carefully listened to the outside.

Larissa looked at her uncle with large questioning eyes. Habakuk kept pulling steadfastly and unmoved on the cord of the fan. Pelegrin looked apprehensively ahead. The young lady had such trust in her famous friend that she felt no fear while he was with her. Pelegrin and Habakuk, had already experienced and survived so many different adventures with the count, that they didn't let themselves worry, when it came to unusual situations.

"Should I take a look at what is happening outside?" asked Pelegrin.

At the same instant, the window of the cabin darkened, - a long unearthly monster started crawling through the window. Larissa screamed and fled to Caprioli. Pelegrin jumped with one leap behind a cabinet, Habakuk

pressed himself with balled fists against the door. If the underside of this monster's arm hadn't been covered with fist size suction pads, one could have thought that it was the tail end of a giant snake. The horrible creature entered the cabin. Searching it slithered through the air and got hold of one of the heavy oak chairs.

The chair rose to the cabin ceiling, banged against the bulwark with a loud crack and then smashed on the floor with such force, that it burst into pieces like a child's toy.

Now, Caprioli also got up.

Calmly he put on his monocle and explained:"If I am not mistaken, this is one of the tentacles of an unusually large octopus. Even here, such specimens shouldn't be coming to the sea surface." He backed up one step looked at Pelegrin with a knowing look and added:"Doesn't it look like this beast arrived as if called..?" Slowly he backed towards the door.

Shrill cries, calls for help, shots, the sound of axes and running feet penetrated the deck to the cabin.

"Take my pistols" said Caprioli turning to Habakuk. His bodyguard already had them in his hands.

Carefully, step by step the count, followed by Habakuk climbed up towards the deck. Pelegrin followed some distance behind. Larissa disappeared in her cabin.

The count had barely lifted his head above the hatch cover when he stopped in amazement. A behemoth the size of a mountain slithered across the deck of the "Fantoma", listing this big ship dangerously with its enormous weight. Huge tentacles, some of which held a sailor or soldier entangled, hung over the opposite rail, or swayed searching between the foredeck the bridge and the stern.

In the middle of these tentacles sat an unearthly head with a razor-sharp parrot beak and shiny green basilisk eyes the size of cartwheels. It really was an octopus, but with a size that only exists in sailors stories bragging in a harbour side tavern.

Count Caprioli moved up on deck but stayed in the shadows.

The monster had not discovered him yet.

In the stern, Baba the maid was washing clothes.

Caprioli saw her standing petrified with rolled up skirts and staring with horrified white eyes at this incredible beast. The recently hung up laundry fluttered in the breeze. Lightening fast one of the tentacles flew towards a bed sheet and tore it from the clothe line. With a cry of rage, Baba grabbed a bucket full with boiling water and poured it over the tentacle. The beast screeched in pain like a rusty door hinge, swung the injured tentacle high in the air and flapping, dunked it in the ocean.

However this tentacle, with its erratic movement, had brushed against the chicken cage which fell on deck and broke. A splendid rooster fluttered to the rail and announced his freedom with a loud cock-a-doodle-doo.

Then, unbelievably and typically of the chicken world, he jumped down placed himself smack in the middle of one of the tentacles and cool as a cucumber started pecking at it. The floor under his clawed feet started moving violently, the rooster, frightened with flapping wings and loud clamour flapped across the deck. But he didn't get far. Faster than the eye could follow, the octopus swung another tentacle around, grabbed him and with feathers and all made him disappear down his throat.

A movement attracted Caprioli's attention towards a large rolled up sail on the opposite bulwark. Carefully the messed up head of the captain appeared.

His eyes were glassy with horror. Groping, one of the tentacles slid in his direction. Bull could not suppress a cry of horror. He had no choice but to jump over board to escape the slithering tentacle – but even in the water he would not be safe from the beast.

Desperately he looked around for help and saw Caprioli in the shadows. The skimpy remains of his hair stood up in anger. With a great leap, which almost made him loose his balance, he jumped over the sail and onto the open deck. In his fist he held a heavy boarding axe.

"Only cowards hide! A captain saves his ship or dies with it!" he screamed at the count. With big strides, the axe held high, he rushed at the lurking octopus. From out of nowhere a tentacle appeared in front of Bull, rapt itself around his stomach, lifted him high in the air and then dragged him from bow to stern through the water.

Then the tentacle slithered up the main mast, until it was higher than the top and swayed the dripping and squeaking captain back and forth like a baby, 20 meters above the deck. For fright Bull had dropped the axe.

Caprioli shaded his eyes with his hand, looked up at the captain in the dizzying height and pondered. The beast became aware of the movement of his shadow. Wantonly and slowly it pulled out the tentacle that was still hanging in the port hole of the cabin and pushed it groping towards Caprioli.

The count seeing the danger whispered to Habakuk who stood behind him on the stairs:

"Quickly bring me the heavy rider's pistols, but double load them!"

Habakuk disappeared but returned a few moments later and handed the heavy weapons to his master with a grin.

"Each one has 2 bullets and triple powder!" he whispered.

Caprioli reached behind him, took the pistols, cocked them, reversed them holding both in his right hand by the very end of the barrels and stretched out his arm. The tip of the tentacle with the deadly suction cups was only a few paces away from Caprioli.

The count stood still as if he were carved in wood. Feverishly he searched for another possibility to save the ship and the people in it. There was temporary safety in the belly of the frigate, but sooner or later, the giant octopus would embrace the ship with its huge tentacles, crush it like a matchbox and drag it into the depth. Only a cannon ball could have penetrated this thick leathery skin.

The tip of the tentacle now groped directly in front of Caprioli's toes. The huge glistening eyes of the beast were wide open, not to miss the tiniest movement.

The instant the tentacle touched Caprioli's shoe, the count extended his arm with exaggerated movement and presented the pistols to the beast. Like lightening the tentacle shot forward to grab the pistols and Caprioli opened his hand. Like before with the rooster, the pistols went straight down his gullet. In an instant a terrible explosion ripped his head apart. A shiver went through the mighty tentacles and they slowly released their prisoners. The tentacle that was high up the mast sank down like a dead leaf, depositing captain bull, unharmed, except for various cuts and bruises on deck.

Caprioli dabbed his fore head with a silk handkerchief, straightened his jacket and turned to Habakuk.

"Well, we managed to accomplish another one, my old friend. I would have never credited this beast with so much intelligence. To kill itself was the most sensible thing to do; it was after all a nuisance here."

To clear the remains of the monster, was a job the count could confidently leave for the sailors and soldiers, who slowly came out of their hiding places.

The sharks received an unexpected feast.

AN ADVENTUROUS BEAR HUNT

The rescue from the giant octopus was celebrated not only on the ""Fantoma"", but by all sailors and soldiers in the fleet, thanks to the count who had treated every ship with an extra small cask of rum.

High spirited laughter mixed with the sound of clinking glasses could be heard in the commanders' cabin on board the ""Fantoma"", where uncle Cyps and Larissa toasted each other. In between the careful and slightly raspy voice of Pelegrin, Habakuk's deep bas could be heard. Coxswain Nieselpriem's laughter sounded like the cooing of pigeons, where as Borromaus, the gunnery officer only grunted occasionally, preferring to concentrate on the glass in front of him.

A bit apart from the others, but carefully watched by the concerned eyes of Larissa, stood Bilg who cautiously sipped the unfamiliar liqueur. Caprioli had insisted that he too should join in the celebration.

Captain Bull however sat alone in his cabin and tried to drown his immense anger in a torrent of brandy.

Instead of being a hero, he was made to look ridiculous – by an *octopus!* And on top of that in front of the count! That was too much. Brooding, he thought about revenge.

In Caprioli's cabin, the wine was heating up the mood more and more. Jokes flew back and forth and laughter rewarded every apt reply. Unexpectedly Larissa turned to Caprioli.

"Uncle Cyps" she begged "Uncle Cyps, to celebrate the day, please, please tell us a story!"

She looked at him in such a way, that he self-consciously stroked his beard.

"I just told you a story!"

He pinched her cheek and pretended to be angry, but Larissa quickly stood on a chair and gave him a kiss.

"Oh yes, count a story please!" begged even Bilg. The gunnery officer growled:

"There is no shortage of adventures in your presence count and I heard more than enough stories of your incredible adventures; but for a story, told by you, I would even sacrifice one of my canons!"

Caprioli laughed.

"Hopefully not one of ours! But I'll make it cheaper. Let's all sit down. I just remembered an adventure were the rescue was completely unexpected and in the last minute, just as with the octopus."

Comfortably the count started to tell his story:

"My old friend baron Lieven and I were out hunting for a stag. It was a strong thirty-six pointer. I never again saw such a magnificent animal.

We were in a raised hide since the crack of dawn, waiting for this majestic animal.

Not a leaf stirred.

Suddenly the stag emerged from the forest and carefully looked around before he started to peaceably feast on the dew dampened grass. Neither my friend nor I dared to disturb this peaceful setting with a shot.

Suddenly the stag threw up its head and stormed off back to the forest with huge strides. Soon after, we saw the reason for his flight: a huge bear ambled, growling through the bushes, sniffing lustfully at bees swarming near the crown of an oak tree.

Surprised, I took a step backwards – catastrophe: crashing, I broke through the rotten floor of the hide and landed in the grass. Luckily I didn't hurt myself, but my rifle was stuck in the tree. I pulled out my hunting knife and saw the bear coming at me fully upright. With a swipe of his paw he knocked the knife from my hand and pushed me backwards to the ground. In the next moment the bear was standing above me with open jaws. Full of fear I saw his dagger like teeth and red tongue. His hot breath blew in my face. All I had for defence were my two hands. In mortal danger, I grabbed the thick fur on his belly and held on with all my might. Immediately he raised his head and started a peculiar howling. I griped his stomach fur harder and he laid back his head even further. His howling became a squeaking. At the same time his right rear leg started to tremble. Now I knew how to interpret this howling, and I had a glimmer of hope: the bear was ticklish!

Wait, old friend, and now I'll really show you, I thought to myself! I burrowed both hands deeply into his fur and started to fondle his paunch artfully and with force. The bear let out a sobbing roar and through himself on the back like a dog. Immediately I jumped up, knelt on the bear and continued my work so artfully that the bear started yowling so loudly that he must have been heard miles away. At the same time he started to struggle so much that I could barely hold on. I must have accidentally touched an especially sensitive spot as the bear started sobbing, coughed, convulsively pulled up his back legs and started to laugh so loud that I thought my ear drums would burst.

Now I put both my hands on this sensitive spot, fondled and tickled till the sweat started running down my fore head. But this became even too much for the bear – I could hardly hold back the laughter myself. Right in the middle of this fine tickling session, he let his head fall to one side, stretched out all paws and didn't move.

I had tickled him to death!

I just wanted to get up on my shaky legs when cracking and crashing timber made me look up. My friend Lieven had also fallen through the rotten floor of the hide. He didn't suffer any damage but rolled on the ground from laughing, gulped for air and held his stomach as if I had tickled him and not the bear. When I approached him he defended himself with arms and legs shouting:"Go away! Go away!"

I had to wait for at least an hour, before he recovered enough and we could speak to each other sensibly. How could I have guest his nature? He was so ticklish, that he had to laugh as much as the bear, just from watching.

The stag was lost this time. Instead, we ended up with game that we hadn't earned in an exactly huntsman like but rather unusual manner we would never have thought off.

We had to leave the bear till the next morning.

We dragged ourselves back to our cabin with hurting limbs; my friend was lame and ill from all the laughing and I from all the tickling work.

"I won't go hunting with you again soon, it's too dangerous." said my friend before going to sleep, but he didn't carry out his threat.

THE WONDROUS THROW

Caprioli quietly stroked his goatee with three fingers of his right hand as was his habit. The little party was beside itself from laughing. Borromaus was holding his aching stomach, Nieselpriem kept wiping his eyes and nose and Larissa's' laughter rang over Habakuk's deep bas.

Bilg called out:"That was a fantastic idea count. If we have another adventure with a monster, then I will also tickle it to death!"

"Be careful young man" warned the Caprioli, "most monsters can't be taught to laugh!"

Pelegrin hardly participated in the merriment. Smiling quietly, he took notes of his masters' story, to enter it in his diary later on. Lifting his head he modestly said:"Some time ago, count, you promised to tell me the story of how with your bare hand you threw a slug at a flock of ducks and downed them all. This story is still missing in my collection, as I was indisposed at the time and could not go with you.

"Yes, yes tell us the story!" the little assembly cried out in chorus.

"All right then, because this is a very special evening and this is a relatively short story, I will tell you what really happened then." agreed Caprioli.

Wittily he began:

"I am always asked where the beautiful heron feather, that I have had in my three cornered hat since my hunting days with my friend Lieven, came from. This is what happened: One day I was standing in the reeds at the edge of a lake hunting wild ducks. I had just downed a beautiful drake and my hunting dog Senta jumped into the water to retrieve him.

With a slug in my hand, I was about to reload my rifle, when a gorgeous silver heron flew over me. My shot had obviously disturbed him. Immediately the hunting fever got to me so strongly that droplets of perspiration started forming on my forehead. However my rifle wasn't loaded yet and I weighed the slug in my hand.

A bold thought entered my head: I raised my arm, aimed and hurtled the slug whistling through the air, at the magnificent bird. My shot was so accurate that it separated the head from the body. The head with the magnificent feathers fell right at my feet. I carefully stowed it in my hunting bag. About one hundred paces further, the body fell into the reeds. Then, this time behind me I heard a whirring sound and saw a flock of ducks lift off from the reeds. My riffle loaded I turned, but it was no use as the birds flew away from me towards the horizon. Longing, I looked after the birds, when suddenly the first bird in the flock fell into the lake as if hit by lightning, followed by the next one and the next one and so on, until all seven were floating dead in the lake. At the same moment I heard a buzzing sound and felt a slight slap in my hand. What was in my hand, but the slug with which I had hit the heron! My hunting fever and my throw had been so strong, that the slug had travelled right around the world and landed exactly back at its origin. Shortly before it landed in my hand, its force was still great enough to penetrate the flock of ducks flying directly in its path.

I never again experienced such a successful hunt – nor one as economical.

"Wow!" The gunnery officer shouted, when Caprioli ended his story with an impish grin in the corner of his eyes, stroking his goatee.

"Around the whole world..."whispered Nieselpriem with a loose lower lip? His hand drew a circle, as if moving around an invisible ball. He didn't comprehend.

Behind the huge Habakuk a chortling laughter – that was Bilg.

"But uncle Cyps...! Larissa squeaked with delight.

"Well yes, that's how it was" said Caprioli "I took the heron feathers as a hunting prise and had them made into a decorative finish for my hat. You have all admired it before and the ducks were devoured by my friend and I that same evening. One can't ask for more proof than that."

For a second he looked at Larissa's eyes, sparkling with exuberance, thought, went to one of the closets searching amongst his possessions. He returned with a beautifully finished clasp which held the gossamer head feathers of a heron.

"I can see in your eyes that you still don't believe me even after all the proof" he said to the girl. "Here are the head feathers of a heron which I have carried in my luggage since those hunting days, waiting for an opportunity to make a lady especially happy. Here Larissa, I give it to you!"

The pretty girl took the feathers with shaking hands and glowing eyes.

"Thank you uncle Cyps... I believe you – in almost everything!"

STRANGE FRIENDSHIPS

Larissa's' excursions through the big ship became more frequent. Sailors and soldiers became used to this and treated her with rough but warm respect. In reality, she was only looking for opportunities to chat with Bilg, who was only slightly older than her. Something about this drummer boy was mysterious and she wanted to find out the reason.

Bilg, was in the lowest gun deck practising his drum roll, where the only thing to disturb were the cannons. Now, he packed up his drum and drum sticks to carry them to his hide out underneath the crew's quarters. He met Larissa on the dark stairs.

"What are you doing here, miss?" he asked surprised. "The only things down here are darkness, rats and me."

"Show me where you live, Bilg" she asked.

Defensively he answered:

"Oh no, miss Larissa, this is not for you. It will give you the creeps -, a cabin boy does not live in a cabin."

Again Larissa wondered about his way of speaking, which didn't belong to a person in his position, his intelligent looking face and his posture.

"Show me anyway, I am not afraid" she insisted.

"But the rats...?"

"With you, I am not even scared of rats."

"Alright, I'll show you something special then, but be careful, the steps are steep."

They descended below the gun battery, felt their way along the store rooms filled with powder kegs and cannon balls, past the armoury and the store room.

In the furthest corner, at the end of a long row of water barrels, was Bilg's camp. He searched in the dark, struck a flint and lit two tallow candles which he stuck to the floor.

"Come, sit here on my crate, miss," he invited her.

She sat and curiously looked around in the flickering light, but other than a rumpled straw bag she saw nothing.

"Where do you keep your things?" She inquired.

Bilg laughed.

"In the crate you are sitting on, a sailor is not allowed to have more. But pay attention now and don't get frightened." trying to distract her. He whistled quietly through his teeth. Immediately there was a barely audible rustling and in the glow of the light Larissa saw two, three large rats. Bilg extended his hand to them. They sniffed his fingers with their delicate noses, jumped on his hand, scurried up his arm and sat on his shoulders. He fished a bread crust from his pocket, broke it into small pieces and started to feed the rats.

Larissa watched with open mouth.

"I have never seen a rat before" she quietly said after a while, "but everyone says that they are repulsive creatures."

"Are they really repulsive...?

"Maybe not Bilg once you get to know them, but I would choose something else to play with."

"I don't play with them miss Larissa, the rats are my friends. When one is all alone, one can even learn to be happy with rats."

The grey animals finished eating the crust. "Shd!" whispered Bilg so low that it was no lauder than a leaf scraping along a wall. Like shadows the rats disappeared.

Bilg sat on a straw bag and stared into the candle flames. Larissa didn't have anything to say either. Suddenly Larissa reached for the fine gold chain around her neck, withdrew a locket and handed it to Bilg.

"There, have a look that was my mother..."

Bilg knelt in front of her, carefully took the small ivory image in his hand. It showed a beautiful and sophisticated lady with slightly foreign features. He turned it over and in a low voice read the engraved inscription.

"You can read...?"Said Larissa surprised.

Bilg looked at her.

"I don't have a mother any more either" he said evasively. "Mine died when I was still very young."

"And your father...?

Bilg shrugged his shoulders.

"I don't know, I am searching for him."

"Is that why you became a cabin boy...?

Bilg nodded.

"I ran away from home."

"Where is your home?"

"Oh, far away – near Trieste. But you wouldn't know where that is."

"Oh yes, I do" answered Larissa eagerly, "I was there once – with relatives at the 'Fontoroso' castle, I was a child then.

Bilg looked at her flabbergasted, pressed his lips together and slowly stood up.

"Let's go miss; I am due on watch by the deck cannons." He said.

Larissa took his hand.

"Will you call me Larissa in future?" she asked.

"Yes, but only when we are alone. It wouldn't be good for the adults to find out", he answered quietly. He carefully guided her up the stairs.

NATAS SCHEITANOFF

Caprioli couldn't get the 'invisible passenger' that Bilg had talked about out of his mind. All he had found out from the young man is that he saw him through the keyhole of a particular cabin which turned out to be uninhabited. It was odd though, that a rumour had circulated not just among the soldiers and sailors of the ""Fantoma"", but also the crews of the other ships, that here and there an 'invisible passenger' had been sighted; however, every time someone tried to catch him, he disappeared.

He decided to ask Larissa. Her expression instantly became serious.

"Yes uncle Cyps, I did see a man, a small ugly man. He stood by the railing, after you and Habakuk were back on board after your ride on the shark", she said.

"Maybe it was a sailor, they are not all exactly good looking", he demurred.

"This man wore a bright red tuxedo with gold embroidery!"

Caprioli quietly whistled through his teeth.

"And he was transparent, as transparent as a window pane."

"You didn't see a ghost by any chance...?"

Larissa pouted.

"My black Baba can see ghosts!"

"And you...?

She thought for a while.

"Actually not. Only sometimes during the night, you know uncle Cyps, then..."

"Wasn't it creepy when you saw the transparent man?"

"Oh, actually not, you are here on the ship."

Bilg also only had vague descriptions to relate.

"He is rarely in the cabin, he is not on the other ships either and yet, suddenly he is there, like a, like the..."

"Like the ship's kobold?" Caprioli helped him and tousled his blond hair.

"I often saw him through the key hole."

"And why did you never tell me?"

"I didn't want to be ridiculed count."

Caprioli lifted his chin.

"And what does he look like?"

"Sometimes he is completely green and transparent... and then only his head is there, floating back and forth with nothing else visible. Sometimes you can't see him at all, but know he is there reading because the pages turn on their own."

"What does he read?" Caprioli wanted to know.

"Oh, all kinds of weird things." Bilg said scornfully. "There are many pages all written in red ink. He is always studying them as if he wants to learn them all by heart. When he is finished, you can sometimes see him roll up the pages and stuff them into a bag.

"Do you understand this, Bilg...?" Caprioli's voice had an unusual undertone.

"Not completely with my head, count."

"There are many things that one can't understand with one's head only, my boy."

Bilg said whispering.

"Do you want to see him, count? A few moments ago he was in the empty cabin..."

"*Now,* in the empty cabin...?

Bilg nodded.

Caprioli went to get Habakuk and Pelegrin. The unoccupied cabin was situated at the end of a long corridor in the forward part of the ship.

Caprioli opened the door with a jerk.

Surprised, a man standing near the cabin window turned, reached for two heavy pistols lying on the table and pointed them at the count and his companions.

"Well, well, who would have thought, captain Bull's acquaintance from the 'Golden Apollo' in Amsterdam, returned Caprioli with a smile at the dangerous threat.

"His Excellency Natas Scheitanoff in person, or how would you like to be addressed at the moment?"

"Names are unimportant here, count, my genealogy goes back further than even yours." Was the answer of that hoarse crackling voice. "One more step and I'll shoot!" The shark eyes glowed green and angry.

Caprioli examined the short, stubby man with the wrinkled parchment like face, as if it were a puppet on a string.

"What benefit would you get out of shooting?" he said unperturbed. "You reached for the pistols and in person threatened human beings. You betrayed yourself this way; you know your own rule!"

The ugly man sneered:

"So far nothing has happened to you, you would only grab at thin air if...But it is high time for you to make your exit, even if I have to help you along a bit myself. You are nothing but a waste of time for me!"

He held the pistols tighter.

Still smiling, the count answered:

"Contrary to what you think, now that I have you in my grasp, I may just take it to mind, not to let you make your exit in your usual manner. Wouldn't that be very embarrassing for you...?"

"But I already told you...!"

At that moment Bilg cried out, took a step forward and pointed at the cabin window.

"The ship is burning!" he yelled shrilly.

Natas Scheitanoff, surprised, turned his head.

With a single leap, Bilg stood in front of him and pushed his arms in the air.

Two shots thundered into the ceiling.

In the next moment Habakuk wrapped his arms around him with such force, that crying out he dropped the pistols. Bilg picked them up and handed them to Caprioli who calmly reloaded them and grinning weighed them in his hands.

"That was a little surprise, your honour? What would you think of the idea if I sent you home with two neat bullet holes in you? I can assure you that you would be welcomed with hellish laughter."

Scheitanoff's lower lip quivered.

"You wouldn't dare, count!"

"You think so...? Caprioli asked mockingly. He winked at Habakuk who immediately understood and smirked.

"There is a little game that we learned from the Turks, Scheitanoff", continued Caprioli twirling the pistols.

"Who ever played this game once, didn't forget it quickly, and could learn a good lesson from it.

"Go!" he commanded suddenly and handed his body guard the pistols.

Habakuk had pushed his index fingers into the barrels of the pistols and with an additional shove secured them there before Scheitanoff understood what was happening. The count cocked the pistols and stepped back.

"Well, that's done", he said. "I would suggest that you sit down very carefully, honourable Excellency, and move around very cautiously from now on. Those things on your fingers would be very resentful, if you were to try and free yourself from them."

Habakuk helped him to sit and carefully placed his hands with the pistols on the table.

"To play at being the kobold won't be possible for a while now", said Caprioli from the door. "Food, should you need any will be supplied by your cousins and should you get bored, let me know, I know other games for the likes of you."

"You are a devil count", gritted Scheitanoff, "but the voyage is long and I will play a little game for you soon!"

"Don't forget with your devilries, that you are under human law, as long as you have the pistols on your fingers!" Warned Caprioli and closed the door.

Pelegrin turned the key in the lock, withdrew it and put it in his pocket.

A HEAVY CONSCIENCE

Caprioli was inspecting the batteries with the gunnery officer. Bilg was polishing one of the cannons. When the count looked at him he said:

"Earlier on, I met the captain on the lower gun deck, count. He told me to ask when he could meet with you."

Caprioli laughed.

"The captain? And he asked you to see me?"

Bilg was insulted.

"He would know why he especially sent me, count."

Caprioli touched his shoulder in friendship and sent him to Bull with the message, that he is expecting him.

Snorting, the captain pushed his bulk into Caprioli's cabin and groaning, sat in the offered chair.

"What brings you to me, captain?" Caprioli helped him to start the conversation.

"You have not been very nice to me lately, count", began Bull haltingly.

Caprioli twirled his goatee and ordered Habakuk to pour two glasses of wine.

"Instead of talking about me, wouldn't it be better to think about your actions and say nothing...?

Bull scratched his head. The counts answer confused him. Then forgetting about everything else, he coughed:"The gold, count, the gold is driving me crazy!"

"Don't you love it more than your beatitude?"

The captains chunky hands moved agitated in the air.

"Liberate me from the gold, count; I don't have any peace any more. At night it lies on my chest like a mountain of rocks and during the day it sends me thoughts that aren't mine. I am no angel count, but I am not a murderer either!"

"You came very close to being one."

"I can't explain it, but I had to do what I didn't want to do – since – since..."

"Since you sold yourself at the 'Golden Apollo' in Amsterdam to a peculiar man and in a very old fashioned way signed a particular piece of paper. Is that not so?"

Bull wheezed in desperation and the tear ducts under his eyes turned blue.

"You can do anything count", stammered Bull, "Free me from this gold!"

Caprioli shook his head:"Only you can free yourself from this gold, captain", he quietly answered.

"I will throw it into the ocean...!"

"That wouldn't be of any use to you – it would come back to you; the devil is in his way an honest businessman. There is only one way to free yourself from the gold and that way you have to find yourself. You are a capable captain, do your duty and think. You will find the way."

A hasty footstep in the hall, the door was ripped open and Borromaus stumbled into the cabin.

"Pirates, count!" he reported. "We are alone; the other ships have fallen too far back to help us."

Caprioli stood up and donned his sabre.

Bull, with clenched fists squeeze himself through the cabin door to the outside.

"How many ships Borromaus...?"

"Only one count, but the most dangerous freebooter in these parts! It is the fast "Devil" owned by the Red Corsair."

"How is the wind?"

"It will be windy, a thunderstorm is approaching us."

"Order: ready for battle!"

Borromaus rushed off, and shortly after the trumpet call: 'All hands to the cannons!'

Caprioli pressed on the button that Larissa had pointed out to him. The secret door opened.

"Pelegrin, you stay with the women!" he ordered.

He waved to Habakuk and went on deck.

THE BATTLE
WITH PIRATES

The "Devil" was a brigantine that made a sailors heart sing and every soldier wishing they had her under his feet. Under two fully rigged masts she whooshed along, cutting the waves with her high bow.

One look assured Caprioli that the ""Fantoma"" was ready for battle. Behind every cannon, there stood a gunnery officer and a man with a burning slow match. The sailors stood by the ropes, ready to carry out lightning fast, any manoeuvre ordered. Bull, with a heavy sabre hanging from his belt, was standing on the bridge eyeing the approaching storm. Nieselpriem together with another sailor was controlling the wheel. A breathless and alert silence prevailed over the ship. It will be a tough fight, thought Caprioli. Although the "Fantoma" had twice as many cannons and could fire much heavier cannonballs than the brigantine, the cannon barrels of the pirate ship were much longer and its cannonballs therefore had a longer reach.

A shame about this ship, it should be captured without damage, was the thought that went through Caprioli's mind. But how...?

The first few heavy raindrops slapped on deck. The count looked at the sky; one of the sudden thunderstorms that frequent this region was coming towards them, ready to unleash its violence.

The brigantine was almost within cannon range of the ""Fantoma"". Suddenly it turned and at the same moment all its cannons fired a broadside. But the commander over there, had been in too much of a hurry to wait till his ship had reached the top of a wave, so all the cannonballs went howling high over the top of the ""Fantoma"".

Borromaus swore under his breath. Before it made sense to give the command to fire, the brigantine had turned again and swept away at high speed.

"They want to finish us with their far reaching cannons without giving us a chance to fire and then they will ram us", he growled. And sure enough, making wide turn, the brigantine came back at them.

Caprioli was silent. He was searching for a plan of battle, but nothing came to mind. Leaning against the foremast he carefully observed the manoeuvres of the pirate ship.

Dazzling lightening lit up the black sky.

"Keep the bow of the ""Fantoma"" pointed directly at the pirate!" he called to Bull. The frigate had to show the least amount of attack area to the pirates.

The ""Fantoma"" turned as if it wanted to ram the approaching brigantine.

Once more the pirates fired, but with the unruly waves, the cannonballs didn't find their target; they splashed harmlessly into the sea on either side of the ""Fantoma"", erupting like huge fountains.

With a crash as if the sky was about to burst, a mass of lightning bolts twitched into the sea.

Behind Caprioli, a dazzling flame shot up.

He jumped aside and saw that a small lightning bolt had hit the base of the mast and stuck there. Wildly it twitched back and forth but couldn't free itself.

Caprioli immersed his thick riding gloves into one of the always ready water buckets, with a swift move he grabbed the lightening bold at the tail end and ripped it out of the already glowing timber. For a moment the jet of flame remained in Caprioli's fist, then, in a horrified attempt to escape, it shot skywards. But Caprioli hung on.

"What are you doing...?" screeched the nearby Borromaus in horror.

"You will see that in a moment, no cannon are to be fired!"

Holding the lightning bolt high up in the air, Caprioli placed himself behind the figurehead in the bow.

For the third time the brigantine approached, trying skilfully to approach the ""Fantoma"" on its side, to deliver a full broadside to her beam.

On a raised area on deck of the "Devil", one could see the pirate captain waving his sabre in the air and yelling out his commands.

Caprioli swung the lightning bolt like a whip, aimed and struck with his extended arm. The fire beam shot ahead into the sabre of the pirate – a flame flickered – and were the pirate chief just stood, the wind was sweeping a small pile of hot ash.

All the sailors and soldiers screamed with happiness.

The brigantine turned again, showing the ""Fantoma"" her stern and the two long rows of cannons.

Caprioli swung his lightning bolt – hissing the fire jet shot off – once – twice – and over there on the "Devil" the bronze barrels of the cannons melted like hot wax and dripped into the sea.

For a moment the sailors and soldiers were breathless. Then uncontrolled cheering and they danced around the cannons and masts.

The ""Fantoma"" now tore after the brigantine under full sail. Borromaus could have destroyed her with a single volley, but he waited for Caprioli's order.

The count was still standing in the bow like a horrible and strange being, with the lightning bolt twisting in his fist.

"One shot from the forward canon across her bow!" Caprioli ordered Borromaus. "These characters will get away from us – they are faster than we are!"

Borromaus jumped for the cannon with four helpers. Like thunder the volley travelled across the sea. When the powder smoke had cleared, one could see a white flag going up on the "Devil".

"Go alongside and board the pirate!" ordered Caprioli the captain.

The seaman grabbed the heavy boarding hooks, axes and cutlasses and stormed to the railing.

The "Devil" hove to with flapping sails and the "Fantoma" approached with speed.

SURPRISE ON ALL SIDES

Habakuk stood amidships in front of a mountain of ready to use cannonballs. He picked up a twenty pounder to examine it. It was so heavy that it would penetrate any ship's deck just with a throw.

Borromaus, who could not use his cannons at such short distance, was waiting, leaning against the forward mast. The fight with sabres and pikes was not his thing, but to be part of the action, he placed a number of heavy pistols on the crate in front of him. As always on such occasions he pulled up his trousers and tucked his shirt under his belt front and back. It was the only sign, for those in the know, to betray his excitement. His open eye glowed like black fire, however every so often looked prying at Caprioli. The count was the first person whose mastery he recognised.

The time had come: grating the "Fantoma" came alongside the "Devil". Jeering and yelling the sailors and soldiers threw the boarding hooks over the railing of the pirate ship, pulled it alongside and made it fast. The crew of the brigantine, adventurous characters, stood along the rail with their hands in the air and let themselves be trussed up without resistance. There were twenty four men; they were laid out like potato sacks one next to the other on deck of the ""Fantoma"". Caprioli watched suspiciously and cautiously. As he could not see any immediate threat, he opened his hand and grumbling the lightning bolt shot off after the receding storm clouds.

"Something is not right here, be careful!" he called to Borromaus and Habakuk.

Soldiers brought a white bearded sailor to him, whom the pirates had tied to a mast on the "Devil".

"I am the captain of the "Vlissingen", which these pirates captured" he introduced himself. "My name is Dierk Opzoom."

The man looked trustworthy and Caprioli shook hands with him.

"Welcome captain, it seems this was a rescue in the last minute for you."

The old seaman nodded.

"Yes, the pirates were about to torture me when your ship was sighted."

Caprioli waved to Pelegrin, who cautiously looked out from the passage way leading to the cabins.

"take the captain down to my cabin and give him appropriate refreshments, he will need it." and turning to the freed captain:"Have a bit of a rest, captain and refresh yourself. We will talk to each other a bit later."

"But please come soon Sir, I have important things to tell you!" answered Dierk Opzoom.

Under the leadership of the gunnery officer Borromaus, Caprioli sent a group of soldiers to the pirate ship to inspect it. An order like that didn't have to be repeated twice. Like monkeys they climbed on board and disappeared in its interior. The count was about to go to his cabin to talk with the freed captain when, on the other side a hatch was opened with a great amount of noise. Six heavily armed men hurriedly climbed up on deck and jumped on board the ""Fantoma"".

What happened now only took seconds.

One of the characters, with a long knife in his hand, rushed towards the prisoners to cut their bonds. Habakuk grabbed him, swung him around his head and threw him in a wide arc into the ocean.

Three others stormed to the quarter deck with their pistols to control the ship from there. However black Baba was there, standing in front of her washing trough working on a mountain of clothes for the officers. She was partially hidden behind a structure and only briefly stopped her work when the shooting started. Fighting was a man's thing she thought. Now she saw the bandits running towards the cabins belonging to her masters. That was too much. She shook the foam from her hands, gathered up her skirts, stormed after them and with her bear like strength, grabbed two of them by the scruff of the neck. With an angry shout, she banged their heads together, pushed them defenceless from fright ahead of her and dunked their heads in the soap suds.

Bilg was watching with enthusiasm. Now he rushed towards them and tied up their feet with the ropes he was carrying and with Baba's help tied up their arms. With two mighty kicks to their hind quarters, Baba delivered them next to their already lined up companions.

The other two pirates rushed at Caprioli, whose elegant clothes attracted them. He drew his sabre – two whistling strokes – their belts flew off cut in half – and their wide trousers slid to their feet. The two characters cried out, grabbed for their pants to cover their nakedness and at the same time dropped their weapons. Like a couple of children, Habakuk tucked one under each arm. Because they wouldn't stop to rant and rave, Caprioli gave them a good whack on their backsides with the flat of his sabre. That was enough. They let themselves be bound and join the others.

But now, there was still one pirate missing, because Baba only got the better of two of the three that had run to the quarter deck. Did he hide or did he get to Larissa's cabin? The question answered itself almost at the same time it was asked. With a crash, the door to the cabins flew open, with one leap the pirate jumped out on deck and immediately turned. In his left hand he held a circular plated thick rope soaked with tar. With the right he swung a broad seaman's cutlass with which he desperately tried to defend himself against a slender rapier yielded by Larissa who attacked him like a wildcat. With her free hand she held her skirts. Baba screeched with pleasure, slapped her knee and yelled:

"Ha, Ha, Ho, Ho, give it to him, hit him, stab him, the bandit deserves it!" The man, hardly taller than Larissa, had his long hair tied in a bun on top of his head and decorated with a parrot feather.

Larissa was ten times faster with her rapier than the pirate. To every one's surprise, although she cut his blouse into shreds, she never injured him. It only took a few hits to defend the attacks of the pirate, the rest whistled flat on his chest, arms and legs, giving him so much pain that he howled like a puppy.

Before Caprioli could intervene, she drove the character against the aft mast, lunged, and drove her rapier through the top knot of the pirate nailing him to the mast. She let go of the rapier leaving it whipping up and down in front of his nose. Believing he was already dead, he dropped his sabre and the tar soaked rope. What still needed to be done, Habakuk finished in next to no time.

Caprioli saluted his godchild with his sabre.

"Look at that, even the art of fencing is taught in the Parisian ladies colleges. Nice surprise!" He said laughing.

Larissa blushed with pride.

"Actually not in the ladies college, uncle Cyps. My father had me taught fencing and a number of other manly arts. I didn't learn how to knit though", she confessed.

Caprioli laughed and nudged the tar rope lying on deck with his foot. Sailors and soldiers approached curiously.

"Greek fire", explained Caprioli, "pitch, sulphur, tow and a few other nice things. This devilish thing burns even better under water than in the air. If this bandit would have been able to light it, the ships and all of us would have been lost, because that fire can't be extinguished. Habakuk take it to my cabin, one never knows what it could be useful for."

The captain of the by the buccaneer's captured "Vlissingen", an honest man, explained how the disaster came about:

He had set sail two months before from Rotterdam with two other three masters of the Dutch-West

Company with freight for Paramaribo. He was set off course during a storm and captured by the red corsair about two days sail from here. The pirates had their hide out on a small island which was not marked on any chart.

Caprioli had listened quietly. Now he sent Habakuk to ask the captain to join him right away.

Bull was still beside himself at how, in just a few minutes, the count had captured the dangerous pirate ship without a battle. The respect he had for him was now, as great as the fear of his smiling cold bloodedness. Now he stood, unsure of who was standing in front of him – a stranger. Caprioli told him in a few words what he had heard from the captain of the"Vlissingen".

Surprise and happiness at not only standing in front of the famous count Caprioli, but also having been saved by a ship belonging to the same company and heading to his planed destination, made captain Opzoom's knees weak. He had to sit down again.

Bull placed a hairy paw on his shoulder.

"Your hair has become white, but if I am not mistaken, you are the same Dierk Opzoom, who twenty years ago was my boatswain on the "Volendam" and I had to fish out of the water in the last minute.

The strange captain eye balled Bull with disbelieving astonishment.

"Then you can't be anyone else but the English cabin boy Frank Bull, who once smuggled a dead rat into my hammock and whose backside I had spank in return!" he said slowly.

"I can still feel the end of the rope today", laughed Bull with a bouncing belly. "But how come we never crossed paths even though we work for the same company?"

"I spent all these years in the south pacific", answered Opzoom, "this was my first command for the company and very likely the last."

"It's not the end of the day yet, my dear captain", Caprioli calmed him. "But now we have to discuss what we have to do next, gentlemen!"

THE CARGO OF THE "VLISSINGEN"

Forty two men from the crew of the "Vlissingen" were found tied up in the cargo hold of the brigantine. They were more dead than alive. The pirates had brought them along to occasionally entertain themselves in their way and then throw them over board. They were taken aboard and distributed amongst the ""Fantoma"" and the four other ships which had come alongside in the meanwhile. There they were properly cared for.

Beside Bull and Dierk Opzoom, the count also invited the captains from the other ships to attend the discussion.

The captain of the "Vlissingen" claimed that he could find the illusive hide out of the red corsairs; it was a small island with a well hidden but sheltered bay. With a bit of luck he was hoping to get his ship back. Further he reported that he had seen masses of cannons and cannonballs from captured and gutted ships. Were the pirates kept their loot he couldn't say, as he was taken prisoner and put on board the "Devil". Eleven men from his crew had lost their lives in the battle with the pirates.

The council of war was soon over.

The pirates' brigantine was according to the law of the sea a prise now belonging to the Dutch-West Indies Company. Under the temporary command of captain Opzoom and a small crew selected from the other ships, she was to become the sixth ship in Caprioli's fleet sailing to Paramaribo. The prisoners were put into chains and for safety distributed among the frigates. The most important task however was to capture the pirate nest before continuing their planned journey. With the cannons of four mighty war ships and five hundred soldiers, not counting the sailors, the venture shouldn't be all that risky, even if there were more pirates on the island.

The fleet sailed closely together with the "Devil" as lead ship, commanded by Captain Opzoom.

Two days later, well away from any of the regular shipping routes, a small rocky island appeared: the pirates' island.

At Caprioli's command the fleet disbursed into a star formation so that the island was covered from all sides.

Carefully the "Devil" stalked the island with reefed sails. After a few hours, Opzoom found the entrance to a quiet and well protected bay – the would be harbour that he had reported. Ready for battle and any surprises they might come across the ""Fantoma"" followed. Now the two ships were next to each other and two hundred eyes searched the beach and cliffs – nothing. There was no sign of life. Half destroyed and wedged into the rocks wrecked boats and empty kegs were the only sign of any human presence. But where were all the cannons and cannonballs that captain Opzoom had talked about...?

At Caprioli's order the heavy anchor chains rattled through the hawse pipes and boats were lowered. The island has to be carefully searched.

Captain Bull remembered that there was a spring nearby to renew the ships water supplies and make the continuing journey easier.

Larissa and Bilg were listening to the discussions between Caprioli and the ships officers.

The first boat took the count, Bilg and Habakuk ashore. Captain Bull sat grimly at the tiller. Nieselpriem followed in the second boat with six heavily armed soldiers.

Borromaus was fuming as he had to stay behind to command the ships.

The island was a wasteland inhabited only by seagulls and other sea birds. Under white clouds they circled over the men stumbling through the rocky terrain; their loud screeching made it almost impossible to communicate, other than shouting to each other. There was no sign of any human habitation. It appeared that the pirates always lived aboard their ships and only occasionally visited the island for some dark unknown reason.

Caprioli had decided to question the prisoners before his departure to discover their secret. Hundreds of bird eggs lay in flat nest between the rocks brightening the sombre faces of the sailors and soldiers. When they also found a crystal clear spring, all their misgivings evaporated.

Caprioli did not give up. Even if the pirates had sunk all the captured ships, he felt that there must at least be some traces of the large "Vlissingen".

Followed by Bilg and the wheezing captain, Caprioli continued to climb up the rocks.

He left the sailors and soldiers to collect sea gull eggs in the meanwhile.

Suddenly Caprioli stopped and smelled the air.

"Can you smell it?" he asked Bull and Bilg, "I don't know, but somehow this odour seems familiar." They sniffed again.

"My name is not Bull if it doesn't stink of cheese, ordinary delicious Dutch cheese!" growled the captain.

"Cheese...?" laughed Bilg, "from where would cheese be coming from on this island?"

"It really does smell of cheese", confirmed Caprioli still sniffing, "I wouldn't know what else could smell of cheese, other than cheese."

They continued crawling through the cliffs on hands and knees, always following their noses. Behind a large boulder which had obstructed their view, they found the answer to the puzzle. Cut deeply into the island a wide bay opened in front of them. Wedged in by rocks and washed by the surf they saw a large merchant ship. Hundreds of cheese balls were strewn amongst the rocks and hundreds more quelled out between the broken hull planks.

It was the "Vlissingen"!

But why did captain Opzoom not mention anything about his unusual freight?

Silent and amazed, the three looked at this unexpected godsend.

"This is a wonderful discovery, Bull!"

Caprioli was the first to find words. "Cheese is healthy, and with this one, you don't even have to hold your nose if it's not present in large quantities like here."

"And the cannons over there are nothing to be sneezed at either!"

Bull pointed at a huge heap of neatly stacked cannon barrels of all sizes. "We could even re-arm the "Devil"; he said thoughtfully, "Borromaus will be very cranky when he finds out what we discovered!"

A boat shot out from behind the "Vlissingen"; Sailors carefully tied it up on the rocks. It was captain Opzoom, who couldn't stand waiting on board the "Devil" any more and had set out on a search for his ship.

He had excused himself from Caprioli's invitation to join him, because he thought it was more important to do a thorough search of the "Devil". What he was looking for, he kept to himself.

The three walked over to him.

The white haired captain was shocked. Barely able to utter a word he examined the wreck of his "Vlissingen".

"Did you have other cargo than the smelly one?" Caprioli asked jokingly, to distract Opzoom from his sombre thoughts.

"Yes, an irreplaceable cargo", was his grim answer. "The wretches left the cheese behind because they didn't know what to do with it. I have to get on board the "Vlissingen" to search."

"With these breakers it will be almost impossible to get on board", said Bull while examining the lay of the wreck and the waves.

"Nevertheless, I have to try."

"No matter what, we will transfer all the cheese wheels that are still in good condition to our ships", decided Caprioli.

Bilg was sent back to get the crews and boats.

THE CHEESE BATTLE

The breakers foamed around the stern of the "Vlissingen"; the bow of the great ship lay in almost calm water. After an inspection from the boat, it was evident that the "Vlissingen" had a very large hole there. It was possible to enter there without danger and salvage the cargo.

Caprioli ordered to bring the "Fantoma" and the brigantine as close as possible to the wreck and anchor them there. Soon boats loaded to the brim with cheese made their way to the ships.

In the meanwhile, captain Opzoom spirited from one section of the ship to the next, but still, no one knew what he was looking for.

After a few hours the "Vlissingen" was almost completely unloaded; the cheese balls were piled up high on the decks of the "Fantoma" and the "Devil"; they were to be distributed amongst the other ships and stowed in the cargo holds later on. The fresh water supplies had also been renewed and the cook received hundreds of sea gull eggs to look after.

Caprioli and Captain Bull, perched on top of a cliff, had supervised the zestful labour of the sailors.

Suddenly, a warning shot boomed across the water from one of the ships on guard.

A salvo of many cannons thundered in reply.

Firing, a brigantine glided out to the open ocean from a hidden bay of the ragged island. It looked exactly like her sister ship which had been captured in such an unusual way and now lay peacefully alongside the "Fantoma". It was obvious that her captain had been waiting for an opportune moment to escape. But he did not count on the determination and self-sufficiency of Caprioli's captains. In no time had the folded sails been unfurled and the four frigates sailed off to capture the fugitives.

What was odd, that the "Imago", the one that had fired the warning shot, kept firing from her stern cannon? It seemed that her captain was trying to warn Caprioli of an invisible danger.

The count who had watched the surprising events with keyed up attention, waved to Bull.

"To the ships!" The captain's voice carried across the waves like a storm and shooed the crew to their boats.

Caprioli immediately ordered to raise the anchor and get the "Fantoma" ready for battle. The defenceless "Devil" was to remain in the bay till the coast was clear. The sails of the four pursuing ships already looked like small white clouds on the distant horizon. Now and then one could hear the rumbling of cannons in the distance.

"Sadly, they will shoot the brigantine to bits and not escape damage themselves", said Caprioli regretfully to captain Bull. The captain growled into his trimmed beard:

"The Austrian gunnery chief Bichler is over there on the "Imago" and with his bow cannon – he calls "The long Lisa" he is just as accurate as Borromaus. I don't think he will let this prize go, if he can."

The "Fantoma" slipped out of the bay and started to sail around the island to investigate every entrance. Caprioli took the spyglass from Pelegrin's hand. A particularly rugged area had caught his attention. At that moment, a third brigantine slid out to the open sea. She had been expertly hidden behind a headland. The name "Hell" was painted in large red letters on her bow.

"Now we know why the "Imago" kept firing those warning shots!" said Caprioli, "from our bay this ship would not have been visible."

He noticed that the "Hell" tried to escape in a wide arc in the opposite direction to her sister ship. Still, something forewarned him in her movements; her captain was trying to get an overview. Was he looking for something?

The "Fantoma" swept like a ghost ship through the waves behind her and the "Hell" had very little chance to escape. "Let her go, count", growled Bull, "You can see she also has the extra long gun barrels. If we get too close, she will shoot us to bits before we can get a single shot off. This time you don't have a lightning bolt to hand!"

As if he had a sudden thought, Caprioli stroked his chin and looked at the captain.

"No, I don't have a lightning bolt, but…"

He did not continue, he fondled his beard and hid an impish smile with his hand.

"I have to speak with Borromaus, Bull", he said. Hurriedly he descended the narrow staircase to the deck.

"I would like to know who cast these long barrels for the pirates. Again, we won't get to fire our cannons, count." Borromaus' voice was rougher than usual from anger.

Caprioli grinned.

"I think it depends on the hits, dear friend."

"If I want to hit, then I have to shoot."

"Of course, the question is with what!"

"With what? What do you mean, with cannonballs naturally?"

Caprioli smiled.

Of course with balls, but not with these heavy ones. Why don't you try it with our cheese balls for once."

"Count...!"

The gunnery officer could barely speak from indignation.

"I am serious! There look, I had a feeling about this, the pirates are turning! Soon they will have us in cannon range!"

Borromaus still bristled at this outrageous impertinence.

"Even cannons have their honour, count! Cheese has never been fired from a cannon!"

"Honour lays in success, not in the charge, old friend. You will not kill people with cheese and you won't destroy a ship; but you can win and retain the ship. That is the important point!"

Caprioli's voice took on the metallic tone of command.

"Gunnery chief, get all cannons unloaded as quickly as possible and load every barrel with three cheese balls, but with the normal amount of powder!"

The order flew from one cannon crew to the next like wildfire. The crews laughed but followed the order with the utmost speed, because they knew it came from the "incredible count". Even Larissa didn't hold back and carried some cheese balls. Black Baba, together with the sailors, rolled the heavy iron cannonballs across the deck and back to their storage. Her skirts flowed and her eyes twinkled with enthusiasm.

"Ready for battle!" announced Borromaus to the count. Bilg stood in the middle of the deck, his cheeks flushed, the drum hanging from his neck, the drumsticks in his hand and an expectant look at Caprioli.

The count raised his hand.

A loud trumpet signal and Bilg began his drum roll, the first time in the presence of an enemy.

The "Hell" came rushing in.

The cannons were raised.

But before they finished their turn to fire a broadside, Borromaus' command:

"*Cheese Fire!*"

A salvo thundered from the deck cannons of the "Fantoma" and immediately after another one from the cannon ports.

The effect was terrible. Although the cheese balls survived the firing, the impact on the brigantine was too much. They exploded into thousands upon thousands of pieces and doused the ship with showers of molten cheese bits. The smelly cloudburst gummed up the sailor's eyes and mouths, extinguished the slow matches and covered the deck with a layer of mush where no foothold could be found. The pirates were horrified and could not understand what happened.

Molten cheese dripped from the bridge and the cannon barrels.

But the cannons on board the "Fantoma" were already reloaded.

A second and a third salvo of good Dutch cheese balls exploded and drizzled over the brigantine. The "Hell" became a purgatory for the pirates.

When the smoked cleared, one could see that the whole ship was covered in a sticky and strong smelling cheese mass. The pirates slipped and tripped screaming over each other.

But that was not enough: suddenly a fierce battle started over there. The pirates were attacking each other with sabres and daggers, pistol shots cracked and screaming men were thrown overboard.

"Board them" ordered Caprioli,"quickly or they will set their own boat on fire!"

He pulled out his sabre.

At full speed the "Fantoma" turned and lay alongside the equally fast "Hell". Grappling hooks kept them together, heavy mooring lines flew and clawed ladders dug into the railing of the brigantine.

Odd: a part of the pirate crew greeted the "Fantoma" with cries of joy. But the battle went on.

The giant Habakuk was on fire with his fighting spirit. Standing high on the bridge deck, he had Bilg and Baba hand him one cheese ball after the other and fired them unerring at anything that moved on the pirate ship. Anyone that was hit on the head or chest by one of these bursting cheese balls would slip on the cheese mass and fall, no matter how solid they were on their feet. The pirate chief, noticeable by his colourful attire, tried to find refuge behind a mast. However, in his anger he became careless and threatened Habakuk with his sabre. A cheese ball hit him squarely in the stomach with such force, that he flew backwards through a deck hatch.

One of the crew saw this. He slid, almost swam towards the hatch, slammed the cover closed and locked it with the barrel bolt. Some of the fighters answered with screams of joy in response. Instead of defending themselves, these pirates stretched out their arms toward the "Fantoma".

Their opponents were quickly disarmed, put in irons and shoved aboard the "Fantoma" to join their cronies.

It turned out that the majority of the crew on the "Hell" had been seaman from captured ships and had been forced to serve by the pirates. Their happiness over the rescue was indescribable.

Captain Bull, hoarse from yelling, climbed down on deck and with his swaying stomach set course for his cabin to allow himself a recovery drink. He had to pass by the bridge deck where Habakuk still stood with his supply of cheese balls. The moor did not trust the peace and constantly peered at the deck of the "Hell" to make sure nothing dangerous appeared there.

A violent motion of the ship caused the cheese balls to roll and one of them burst on the captain's head. Outraged Bull looked up, saw the moor standing there and thought he was playing a prank on him. Snorting he searched for something to throw and saw a few cheese balls that Bilg hadn't passed up to his friend yet. With a curse he grabbed one of the balls and threw it up at Habakuk. The moor thinking the captain was playing games caught it with a laugh and smashed it on Bull's head. Fuming with anger, Bull bent down to pick up another cheese, but before he could get up, a third missile exploded against his copious rear end. He screamed like a wounded bull and threw a ball at Habakuk with all his strength. The cheese missed its target. But now Habakuk started to enjoy himself. With a mighty swing he reached for another cheese ball, but instead Baba, who was just passing ended up in his huge fist. Before the moor noticed what he had in his hand and could control his swing, the screeching Baba was hurled towards the Bull's staring face. Like a meteor with flying skirts, her round rear end collided with Bull's face.

It required many buckets of cold water to bring the captain back to life.

Caprioli himself had to defend his body guard against black Baba's violent attacks. From that time on, Habakuk feared her more than the devil himself.

KIDNAPPED TO THE NORTH POLE

In the evening, Caprioli was rowed over to the "Devil", whose gun barrels had been molten by the lightning bolt. Captain Opzoom and all the commanding crews from the captured ships were on board the "Fantoma" to celebrate the second fantastic victory over the pirates.

As the four frigates had not returned from the chase yet, the count wanted to use the time to do a thorough investigation of the pirate ship.

He had just looked around the captain's cabin when an unusual buzz and a slight motion of the ship caught his attention. He walked to the window and saw that the "Hell" was no longer surrounded by foaming green water, but was floating high above drifting clouds.

"How do you like this air travel count?" he heard himself being addressed by a very familiar voice. Caprioli turned around. In a dark corner he saw a poison green shimmer which bit by bit formed the figure of Natas Scheitanoff, but remained transparent.

"Air travel on a sailing ship would be something new, even to you. Shall we bet that even your luck wouldn't help now?"

Caprioli sat down leisurely on one of the leather chairs, placed his three cornered hat on the table and started toying with his monocle.

"How did you free yourself from the pistols...?" he asked examining Scheitanoff from the bottom up.

His Excellency croaked a laugh.

"You will not dupe me again! Good old Bull paid me a visit in my cabin and noticed that you had removed the flints before you had the shooting irons installed on my fingers. Since he was still hungering after his mountain of gold, he had to tell me and I was free. How should I know how pistols that don't fire are made? I am a peace loving being. You, however, even seem to be concerned about the well-being of a devil!"

Caprioli nodded.

"Of course, if you and your kind weren't important, then you wouldn't be here."

A croaky scornful laughter was the answer.

"Then watch the way you will finish with me, unless you should come up with the intelligent thought to ask me for a bit of help..."

Caprioli laughed:"Go home to your grandmother, you haven't even graduated yet!"

A glow of fire like sheet lightening flared through the dimly lit cabin.

Scheitanoff was gone.

The ship descended at high speed, dove into the waves with a swoosh – seconds later it crashed into an obstacle, - sharp grinding sounds along the hull, - glass or wood splintered – the window pane burst.

"Nice mess", Caprioli murmured, "what sort of devilry did this character cook up this time!"

He went out on deck to find out what had happened.

As far as the eye could see a jagged ice surface stretched before him, from which rose blue shimmering icebergs. Behind him he saw the dark sea. The "Devil" must have landed in the vicinity of the North Pole.

The ship had hit the ice with full force, carved a wide channel and then stopped. Carefully he climbed off the ship. He couldn't see any damage, but she was lying lower in the water than normal which made him come to the conclusion that there was a hole below the waterline. The "Devil" was probably being held by the ice mass that she had driven into. It was probably high time to leave the ship and establish a camp on the solid surface as best as one could. What will happen after remains to be seen?

"It is just as well that I like my own company" he said to himself, looking at the white and endless emptiness.

He climbed back on board.

He discovered a bag of dried peas, salt and a mighty piece of smoked pork in the cook's pantry. Amongst the stolen goods in the captain's cabin, he found an artfully sewn Eskimo suit with attached fur boots made from seal skins; the jacket was lined with polar fox fur. In a sea chest that had been used as a bench he discovered a large hoard of whisky bottles.

"One has to be lucky!"

Quickly he searched through the ship, and placed everything he could find to survive without too much hardship on the ice. He didn't forget to take a rifle with a good supply of slugs and powder. As a last thing he carted a good supply of firewood to his camp.

Exhausted from the unaccustomed heavy work, he sat on the ice in the middle of his supplies, started a fire, uncorked a bottle of whisky and took a sip."Brr that stuff tastes good, at least it warms you up on the inside!"

He took another sip and another. The bottle was almost empty but he was still freezing.

"Oh, the Eskimo suit, I almost forgot it!"

He took off his clothes and donned the unfamiliar article of clothing. Its former owner must have been a giant as it fit like made to measure.

One more sip!

He sat on a couple of blankets and leant back comfortably against a small ice berg behind him.

"We'll wait till the next stage coach comes by...!"

His eyes closed and he peacefully fell asleep.

THE POLAR BEAR

It was dawn when Caprioli woke up. He yawned, rubbed his eyes and stretched – he saw the empty whisky bottle lying on the ice...straightened with a jerk and was wide awake. There was no trace of the "Devil" or the wide expanse of ice where he had debarked. Instead of the ice, he saw the black, blue waves of the ocean around him, and discovered that he was floating on a small ice berg island. During the night, the ice surface he had camped on, had broken away and floated off to sea.

"I should have taken sails and a rudder", he thought to himself.

"Incredible what this scoundrel can come up with to kill me. But until now he hasn't got me yet!"

A roaring grumble from the top of the ice berg he was leaning against made him turn and look up.

Partly hidden by the jagged ice, he saw the mighty head of a polar bear peering down at him. The bear must have watched him for a while, but couldn't work out what that strange being was, from which clouds of whisky fumes floated up to it.

Caprioli reached for his rifle and wanted to jump up, but couldn't. The strong drink had warmed him up so much during the night that his rear end, through the blankets, had melted a hollow in the ice. In the cold morning hours, he ended up solidly frozen in place.

Now, there was only one way out of this situation: out of the pants! At the speed of thought, keeping a constant eye on the bear, he undid the belt, slipped out of the leggings and boots to freedom. He grabbed his rifle and jumped with one big leap behind the nearest ice block.

A heart shot was impossible as the body of the animal was mostly hidden by the ice. With bared teeth, the bear kept looking back and forth, from the frozen pants with attached boots to Caprioli. Although the count still wore his stockings and long underwear, he began to feel the cold. Something had to happen. It happened so quickly that in his surprise he forgot to shoot. The bear reared, sat on his haunches, slid down the ice berg with great momentum, straight into the open and welcoming frozen leggings. He landed with such force that the pants tore loose from the ice.

In bear fashion, he stood up on his hind legs, dressed in leggings and boots he immediately wanted to charge at the count. But the smooth soles on the boots slid from under him and bang, he sat on his fat rear end. The bewilderment in the dressed bear was so funny that Caprioli laughed out loud.

Seconds later, the bear stood up again and balanced with open maw and paws towards the count.

Caprioli lifted the rifle, aimed and fired. Click! The flintlock sparked, a long blue flame shot from the count's mouth directly into the bear's face and singed his beard whiskers. The powder in the rifle was wet, but the strong alcohol breath coming from Caprioli's mouth was ignited by the spark.

The bear howled in terror and ran off. Slipping and sliding, the count caught up with him just as he fell, head first into the water. Caprioli managed to grab the boots, and as quickly as the bear had slid into to them and the attached leggings, he was out again. He swam of as if possessed.

How wonderful and warm the leggings and boots were! Peacefully, Caprioli buttoned up the pants.

As his stomach started to growl, he decided that above all it was time to prepare a proper meal. He stacked up some wood, placed the steel tripod over the stack, threw some chunks of ice into a copper pot and lit the fire.

While the fire crackled, he cleaned his riffle, prepared some dried peas and cut off a good chunk of pork.

"I won't starve for the time being", he thought to himself and – with a look at the whisky bottles - "nor will I freeze. So let's postpone the worrying of for a couple of days."

Meanwhile, the ice had melted in the pot and the water was lukewarm. In his mind, he already tasted the wonderful pork in the pea soup. But it was too early to celebrate.

At the edge of his ice island, the mighty head of the bear emerged from the sea. The animal placed its paws on the ice, trying to climb back up. His hunger was greater than his fright. Again Caprioli couldn't shoot. He had to try and frighten the animal away and looked for an object he could throw at the bear's head. He looked at the copper pot with the molten ice. He grabbed it, swung it high and slipped. The water spilled over the paws of the predator.

Surprised, the bear didn't move for a few seconds, but that was enough to solidify the water in the extreme cold and solidly freeze the paws of the bear.

The bear started to push and shove, but in vain. He roared in anger and pulled ever harder. But because most of his body was in the water, he was only able to apply a tiny bit of his strength, and kicked so hard with his legs that the water foamed.

With the rifle in his hand, Caprioli analysed the situation. He could kill the bear with one or two well aimed shots, but now he had another idea.

Quickly, he fanned the flames so that the fire roared. He poured rivers of ice water over the paws of the bear which froze instantly. Soon the animal's paws were covered with a thick layer of ice, and there was no more danger that the bear could break free.

Only then, Caprioli thought of himself and prepared a delicious meal.

The bear kept kicking the water and pushing the island of ice ahead of him in a continuing effort to break free and climb on the ice.

A good slug of whiskey ended Caprioli's meal.

The bear was going crazy from hunger and with his mouth drooling he eyed Caprioli's tall figure. But where on this ice flow could the count find an animal to hunt and feed to the bear?

He played thoughtfully with his rifle.

On the other side of the ice floe he could hear some loud splashing and snorting; no doubt, a large seal had slung itself on the ice. In moments, a loud shot came from Caprioli's rifle, and the animal didn't move any more.

He cut off pieces with his hunting knife and threw a big chunk to the bear. The meat landed near the bear's head but he couldn't reach it.

He raged from greed. In the wish to reach the fine smelling meat, he started to kick harder and lay on his side. The floe started to turn. Yes, this observation deserved another slug, and Caprioli did just that.

With the barrel of his rifle, he retrieved the meat, cut it into smaller pieces and pushed them back to the bear.

With a ravenous appetite, the huge beast devoured them, but his greed made him berserk.

In the meanwhile, evening was approaching. Caprioli took his sea chart and studied the surroundings, if one could call them that, in the dwindling daylight. With the help of the pale shimmering stars and the bright North Star, he could work out the direction he must travel to get back to his fleet. But did the captains wait for him...?

With the barrel of his rifle, Caprioli pushed piece after piece of meat to the bear, but in such a way, that if the paddling bear wanted to reach it, he had to push the floe in the right direction.

ON HORSEBACK OVER THE OCEAN

For many night hours, Caprioli guided his strange craft along the correct course, but then in fatigue he fell asleep next to the second whisky bottle.

As the day dawned, he woke with a strange feeling.

A warm wind was blowing, the waves had the steel blue colour of the South Atlantic, and swarms of flying fish sailed over the water surface. The bear had disappeared.

The only thing left of the ice flow was the rapidly dwindling ice berg and a small quickly melting strip of ice.

It took a few minutes for Caprioli to work out what had happened. The bear had propelled the island much quicker than he had estimated; during the night it had reached the rapid current of the warm Gulf Stream, the ice had melted over the bear's paws, and the ice island was reduced to the small floe that was left.

Only a short time and Caprioli will have to swim.

"If I have no choice but to swim, then I will do so befitting my status", he said to himself.

He took off the Eskimo outfit, put on his own clothes, slipped on his jacket, fastened the belt with his sabre and put the three cornered hat with the beautiful heron feather on his head. He slung his rifle, powder and slug bag over his shoulder, although they would hardly be useful in the water.

With regret he looked at the bag of peas and the bacon, but it was too dangerous to start another fire. Instead he put a bottle of whisky in his backpack and two more around his neck with a bit of string.

This way equipped, he waited till the ice under his feet would melt away.

A strange noise made him listen: snorting – quietly, a gentle whinny, like a loving stallion for his mare…

Horses here in the ocean…?

Truly, there they were:

Three splendid horses of a size never seen before! A stallion and two mares had romped about at the back of the island and in play had come in the field of his vision.

Caprioli didn't want to believe his eyes. The animals' size was the only thing that distinguished them from their cousins on land, except that they had sea-green eyes and long silky eye lashes. He remembered having seen pictures of these, long believed to be extinct and fairy tale creatures, in some very old illustrations.

Caprioli, the old equestrian and connoisseur of horses, was so delighted that he forgot the dangerous situation he was in. The beautiful apple greys didn't seem to have noticed him.

Instinctively he searched through his pockets. Didn't he break of a few pieces from the sugar loaf in the cook's larder? Yes, of course!

He quietly flicked his tongue to attract them. The stallion pointed his ears, scenting, opened his nostrils and trustingly approached. Carefully he sniffed the unknown sugar, licked it and took it with obvious pleasure with his soft muzzle. With a low whinny he called his companions. They also received some sugar and let themselves be stroked behind the ears.

With soft lips, the stallion nibbled at Caprioli's hand. He received another piece and snorted with pleasure.

"I will never go to sea without a good supply of sugar anymore!" Caprioli thought.

The ice on which he stood had melted away to a narrow strip. Peas, bacon, the wood and the Eskimo suit had sunk into the depths or floated away. Now, it became serious. He decided on a desperate attempt at his rescue, and didn't solely rely on his usual luck, but also his riding knowledge. He lured the stallion to him, stroked his nostrils, patted his neck and swung himself gently on his back. The stallion hesitated, whinnied shrilly, reared high out of the water, but Caprioli understood how to quickly calm him to forget his fright before he could shake off the unfamiliar weight. He and his mares received another piece of sugar and all was peaceful. It didn't take long before the stallion let himself be guided with gentle knee pressure; the mares followed high spirited with surprising agility and such speed that Caprioli had to hang on to his hat. Now, he took hold of his mount's mane, chirruped and gave him an encouraging slap. Like the wind, the stallion took off with him; the mares followed snorting behind. Caprioli worked out the direction by the position of the sun.

The horses didn't seem to know fatigue and covered distances in a short time that would have taken days for the fastest sailing ships.

The only annoying part was the many sharks and huge sword fish. They obviously feared the sea horses, but the further south the journey took him and the warmer the water became, the bolder they became. They didn't show any appetite for horse meat, but shot up from the bottom and boldly snapped at Caprioli's legs. Suddenly a huge shark shot by him so closely that its rough skin rubbed against his leg; only the speed of the stallion saved him by a hair. That was too much! As a whole school of smaller sharks was approaching, Caprioli decided on a big sacrifice. He took the two whisky bottles from around his neck, and as another shark's head surfaced next to him, he cracked them together, poured the strong liquid in the water and threw the broken bits of the bottles down its throat. The shark dove to the depth as if possessed. The other sharks however, having the alcohol flowing through their gills, began an erratic dance, jumped out of the water, bumped into each other and in the end, intoxicated, started devouring each other. It looked like a mediaeval farmers feast.

The stallion with Caprioli on his back shot through the waves faster and faster. As the last glowing edge of the sun disappeared over the horizon, the rocky silhouette of the pirate island rose from the sea. He directed his mount into the bay and saw to his surprise, not only his five frigates lying peacefully next to each other, but a duplicate of the with cheese balls captured "Hell" with the name "Death" on the bow. Next to the "Death", lay the undamaged "Devil" with which he had been hijacked to the North Pole.

Caprioli rubbed his eyes, but what he saw was no phantom. He directed the stallion to the "Fantoma", tenderly stroked his neck, and climbed, unseen, up a nearby rope ladder to the deck of the flagship.

The victory celebration over the pirates was still in full swing. Odd, did his adventure really take two nights and a day, or was everything a dream like illusion fabricated by Scheitanoff?

But can one get wet, when one *dreams*, riding through the ocean...?

A CONFUSED SERVANT AND A ROYAL GIFT

Deep in thought Caprioli descended the steps to his cabin, Pelegrin sat at a small desk working on his diary by candlelight. Surprised, he jumped up when he saw his master enter with dripping clothes.

"Did you fall in the water, count?" he asked bewildered. Laughing, Caprioli placed the rifle, powder and slug bags, remains of the booty from the "Devil" on the table.

"If that's not sand dripping from my clothes, than I must have fallen in the water somewhere, and if you haven't seen this rifle somewhere before, than I brought it back from a very solid dream."

Pelegrin didn't understand the count, but still carefully reached for the rifle and examined it.

"That is really a strange weapon, count..." he said slowly.

"Just as I thought! But now bring me a change of dry clothes as quickly as possible."

With small, hurried steps, puzzled and shaking his head, Pelegrin brought new underwear and a dry suit.

"One can't let you alone for a moment, count!" he said disapproving, while helping his master out of his dripping jacket.

Caprioli grinned.

"Be happy that at least one of us stayed dry, and thank God that you don't dream as realistically. By the way, have you ever seen drunken sharks or sea horses, Pelegrin...?"

"You must have caught a cold and you are feverish, count" answered the old servant with concern.

"I hope not, although there are enough grounds. So, you haven't seen any? If we are lucky enough you will be able to admire some in the morning."

"Drunk sharks...?"

Pelegrin raised his eyebrows almost to the beginning of his wig hairs.

"But no, dear old friend, I meant *sea horses,* sea horses with sea green eyes and larger than I have ever seen. You will be able to fill many new pages in your diary."

Pelegrin rubbed the count's feet to warm them and slipped on fresh socks.

"Tomorrow morning you will feel much better, count", he said with his calming old man's voice.

I will make you some mulled wine and let you sweat it out, than you will soon forget the spook about drunk sea horses."

Caprioli sighed.

"The sharks were drunk, dear Pelegrin, not the sea horses. You don't even believe my dreams any more, even with all the proof."

He lay down in his hammock, with great pleasure, slurped the spiced wine which Pelegrin had prepared, let himself be tucked in and soon fell asleep.

The next morning, the captains, with loud commands made sure that the crew made the now grown by three ships, fleet ready for sea. After a short discussion, captains were appointed for the new ships, chosen from the most experienced officers. As the rescued sailors from the "Vlissingen" had now recovered, they were distributed among the brigantines; in addition each one received ten soldiers to help the sailors. The crews rescued from the pirate ships were allowed to rest a bit longer.

The new ships also had to be provisioned with fresh water. Caprioli had the Dutch cheese and collected sea gull eggs evenly distributed. Borromaus and the other gunnery officers managed to re-arm the "Devil" with cannons selected from the huge pirate booty.

As the ships were travelling without freight, the rest of the cannons were loaded also. Investigating sailors found mountains of cannonballs and powder barrels in a cave. These too, were loaded, as they would be very useful at the fort in Paramaribo.

Caprioli's adventures with the polar bear and the sea horses became even more mysterious, as he carefully questioned his officers, if anybody had missed him in the last forty eight hours. They looked at him uncomprehending and thought he was joking. Even Pelegrin didn't notice his absence, and took Caprioli's question as a result of the fever, which, however was not even noticeable from any sneezing.

During the morning hours, Caprioli found out from the pirate captains and their leader, the explanation of how there were constantly contradictory reports from the captains of attacked merchant ships. These captains claimed that they were attacked by the red corsair at the same time but in places that were many sea miles apart. There was not only one red corsair but three brothers with identical brigantines. When these ships travelled at the same time, to rob and plunder, but in different directions, then they all carried the name "Devil"; however if two of them were sent to fool peaceful merchant ships or lure them into a trap set by the real "Devil", then the names "Hell" and "Death" were painted on their bows.

And how was the third brigantine, the "Death" captured? Bjorkr, the captain of the "Imago" and its gunnery chief

Bichler, rubbed their hands together as Caprioli asked them.

"First we organised some big fireworks, but in vain, as we had to stay out of reach of their cannons", explained the white bearded captain. "But then we put all bets on one card and chased them. Before they could fire, Bichler aimed his "long Liesel", fired and bang! The only remains of the "Death's" rudder were a few splinters. The pirate's brigantine was ours. We boarded her, subdued the crew and took her in tow. I had the rudder replaced in the meanwhile."

"You did a fantastic job!" praised Caprioli, "the gentlemen in Amsterdam will have to reach deep into their pockets for this prise."

With a stern look, Captain Opzoom was still searching the captured ships. Time after time he had himself rowed from one brigantine to the next and then back to his "Vlissingen".

Finally, Caprioli couldn't watch the misery of the old man anymore and asked him directly:

"Losing the ship and its cargo was not your fault captain. Tell me, what else did the pirates steal?"

Hesitantly Opzoom answered:

"All the money for the colony, thirty thousand ducats, which was entrusted to me for the governor of Paramaribo. I am a ruined man, count. Even if this tragedy wasn't my fault, no merchant would trust me with another command."

Caprioli whistled in surprise.

That is definitely bad, captain", he said. "Guilt or no guilt, here merchantmen silently include luck in the equation, which is part of any successful business, like amen to a prayer. I don't think that the pirates hid the gold on the island. I am of the opinion that they did hide it on one of the brigantines."

"That's why I searched everywhere, count; I really do not know where to look any more."

A sharp cry and the sound of something heavy falling, interrupted the conversation.

Caprioli and Opzoom quickly approached the railing to see what had happened.

Captain Bull had slipped on a piece of cheese, which had been carelessly left behind, and had fallen through one of the railing loading gates. But he did not fall in the water. His coat collar had snagged on a hook protruding from the hull, and he appeared to have broken his neck from the heavy fall. He dangled there like a lifeless puppet.

Two sailors heaved him up and placed him on deck. Nothing had happened to the mountain of muscle; he had only feinted from fright. After a hefty slug of brandy, he opened his eyes again. Surprised, he looked around, saw captain Opzoom and moaning, pushed himself back on his feet.

"What did you say Dierk, thirty thousand ducats?" he groaned. "Come!"

"I can thank the fine gentleman from Amsterdam for this, I clearly saw how he pushed the piece of cheese under my feet", he said to Caprioli with glassy eyes.

He grabbed the baffled captain Opzoom by the shoulder and dragged him down to his cabin.

Again, Caprioli gave off a low whistle and stroked his goatee with his thumb and index finger while smiling.

He waved to Nieselpriem and ordered him to have the chains removed from twenty of the prisoners, have them guarded by an equivalent number of soldiers and get them to thoroughly clean up the remaining sticky cheese mess from the "Hell".

About two hours later, Caprioli stood in the bow of the "Fantoma", searching the ocean with his spyglass. Soon he discovered what he had suspected; beyond the reach of the unaided eye, he saw white foam trails circling and playfully criss-crossing through the waves, only to begin anew in another spot.

The seahorses!

"With your permission, count, may I ask you a question?" He heard captain Opzoom's voice behind him. He put down the spyglass, turned around and looked at the perturbed face of the old seaman.

Captain Bull stood grinning behind his comrade. Opzoom pointed behind him with his thumb.

"He gave me a large chest filled with gold, exactly thirty thousand shiny new Dutch ducats and said that you would confirm that it was rightfully earned…"

One could see that the old captain thought that it was just a dream.

"Yes, my dear captain, I can confirm that this gold was as rightfully earned as any possession which one hasn't earned, but is still rightfully his" answered Caprioli thoughtfully.

"I don't understand that, count!"

"Think about later. I can reassure you about this gold: It comes from a little adventure that captain Bull and I had some time ago – it is also a prize."

" But who gives away so much money, no rational person would do that!" insisted Opzoom.

Caprioli stroked his chin.

"You can see that it does happen some times. You can confidently take the money, but never ask for the reason behind this regal present, that is Bull's secret and mine."

Opzoom left like someone sleepwalking.

The giant Bull looked at the count with a happy smile.

Caprioli nodded.

"You found the only way by yourself, Bull – now you are free!"

THE PIRATE TREASURE AND AN UNEXPECTED ADVENTURE.

To make loading easier, all eight ships were tied up next to each other.

As there wasn't much to do for Bilg the drummer boy, he decided on his own accord to search the captured brigantines. Pirate ships must have secrets, otherwise they are not, he said to himself. But he wasn't alone.

Larissa had put together a fantastic costume from Bilg's clothes and crawled with her friend, wearing pants and a brightly coloured kerchief over her black hair, through the most hidden corners of the ship.

As Bilg was at home on a ship, Caprioli let them have their fun. It took all his powers of persuasion to calm down the clamouring black Baba. The sailors and soldiers had no time to concern themselves with Bilg and his companion, but quietly snickered to themselves when they saw them.

"These brigantines are especially designed to ram other ships. So, if we want to find anything special, we have to search in the stern, as the pirates wouldn't hide any loot in the dangerous part of the ship", explained Bilg knowingly.

Armed with a lantern, the two of them descended into the dark belly of the "Hell".

Deep under the gun deck, they found a long row of chambers, which held sails, ropes and ammunition for the cannons. One could see that everything had been kept tidy at one point, but that someone had routed around, probably captain Opzoom. The last chamber, right in the stern, was quite large but empty. A narrow set of stairs led upwards directly to the captain's cabin.

The lock for this chamber had been broken.

"If there is something to find, then it can only be here", thought Bilg, the lock was only broken after the capture, because the splinters are still very fresh. Still, it seems that nobody had carried anything away, as there are no footprints in the dust."

Larissa shrugged her shoulders.

"He must have only shone his lantern into an empty room and left. I don't know where else to look, unless, there is a trap door or double wall somewhere."

The ships wall isn't double, one can see that right away", but he checked the floor inch by inch. There was no sign of a trapdoor anywhere.

In the darkest corner of the chamber they discovered a large barrel; it looked like someone had placed it there at some time and it had been forgotten. An old torn fishnet carelessly draped over the barrel, confirmed that thought. A few paces further on, was a ladder with five steps

"Everything on this ship is tidy, except here", said Bilg thoughtfully.

"If I move this ladder against the barrel, I could look inside it", thought Larissa.

"Only herring or pickled pork barrels have a removable lid", informed Bilg, "this one is an old wine barrel with a bung."

Larissa didn't let herself be diverted. She walked up to the barrel and gave it a kick with her toe. There was no sound.

Bilg also walked up to the barrel and tapped it with the knuckles of his fist. No doubt, the barrel wasn't empty.

"There is no wine or other liquid in here either", said Bilg, "look, there is only a bit of twisted rag in the bung hole. Come, give me a hand!"

He put down the lantern and together they pushed the ladder against the barrel.

Bilg picked up the lantern again, climbed up the latter and with effort threw down the net. The barrel was only covered with some loose fitting planks, which were easily pushed aside.

Bilg stared spellbound, with open mouth into the barrel.

"Well, what is in your wine barrel, maybe precious stones?" mocked Larissa.

Bilg remained silent, and searching, swung the lantern back and forth.

"Did you lose your tongue, Bilg?" Larissa was getting angry.

Finally, Bilg turned to his friend and whispered:

"We have it...!"

"What do we have...?"

"The treasure, Larissa!"

"In the barrel? You are seeing ghosts!"

"The barrel is full with gold, Larissa – to the rim!"

He reached in with his hand and let a handful of ducats fall clinking back into the barrel.

Larissa cheered loudly.

"Come down and let me have a look too!" she begged.

To make it easier to climb down the narrow steps, he handed her the lantern. Larissa placed it on the floor and gave Bilg her hand. But the steps were wet; he slipped and pushed the lantern over. The light went out.

"Now, we are in trouble", Larissa said frightened.

"If nothing worse happens...! Bilg laughed. "I know exactly where the stairs to the captain's cabin are, we can easily feel our way there. Give me your hand. What is important, that we have found the treasure. The others will be surprised!"

"Quiet!" whispered Larissa, "Don't you hear anything? Somebody is walking over there!"

They listened, holding their breaths.

Where the dangling door was, quietly tapping steps could be heard through the wooden wall.

The steps came closer.

The dull shine of a lantern was visible through the partially open door, disappeared and reappeared through the slit in the door, as if the bearer was looking for something.

The door was opened further with a low squeak, and an unknown sailor crept in. In one hand he carried a lantern covered with a rag and in the other a long handled heavy hammer. Bilg and Larissa hardly dared to breathe. The man could only be one of the pirates who had escaped. Still, the ship or at least this room must be unfamiliar to him, otherwise, why was he searching along the ship's wall with a lantern? It wouldn't be long before he discovered the two of them – and then there would be a fight. Ready for anything, Bilg crouched down with balled fists, ready to jump. By Larissa's breathing, he could tell that she too wasn't frightened and ready. - Now the light remained in a particular spot, and Bilg saw a heavy steel stud protruding about four feet up from the floor boards.

The man put the lantern on the floor so that the light shone on the stud. Then, he swung the hammer with all his strength at the broad side of the stud.

An almost invisible sliding hatch slid upwards. Swishing, a stream of water flowed into the room.

Bilg cried out from fright.

The man turned, swung his hammer and stared horrified into the darkness. But, before he could react, Larissa jumped at him, like a shot from the dark, head first between his legs. With a gurgling cry, he fell forward and hit his fore head on a corner of his hammer. He lay there unconscious.

Bilg picked up the hammer and with a heavy swing, managed to close the hatch again.

The water quickly seeped into the bilge, through the holes in the floor boards.

Quickly, Bilg tore the rag from the lantern and stood with the raised hammer of the unconscious pirate.

"That was fantastic, Larissa!" he praised his friend.

"Your sword play is incredible – and now this...! I wouldn't have given a girl credit for that!"

"Pft, girl! - What do you know – this was nothing! I bit of the head of a frog once, only for a bet", bragged Larissa.

"Take the lantern and quickly get the net! And then relight our lantern", ordered Bilg.

Larissa dragged over the big net, and they wrapped up the pirate so well, that a spider wrapping up its prey couldn't have done any better. They wrapped the attached towing ropes around him, in such a way that he had no chance of freeing himself when he woke up.

"And now what...? Larissa asked.

"What now! How can you asked such questions? Now, we are going to see the count and tell him everything, but only him, do you understand?"

"That I am not a goose, I already showed you", hissed Larissa.

"I apologise, I didn't mean it that way", answered Bilg.

They took the lanterns and carefully climbed up the stairs leading to the captain's cabin. From there they could easily reach the upper deck again.

HOW THE BRIGANTINES WERE SAVED AND THE GOLD TREASURE SALVAGED.

There was a lot of excitement on the decks of the "Death" and the "Devil" but especially on the "Fantoma". Sailors and soldiers ran back and forth, shouting and gesticulating, as if they were being led defenceless to their doom.

Larissa and Bilg barely heard through the noise:"Help, the ships are sinking...! It's the pirate's work!"

They couldn't have meant the "Fantoma", as she was riding high on the water as always. But the other two brigantines! Frightened, Larissa and Bilg saw that they sat about three feet deeper than normal. The character that they had tied up on the "Hell" obviously had been on the other ships before and had opened the secret hatches. No more time to lose! They rushed across the deck, jumped like feather balls from one ship to the other, till they stood on the "Fantoma".

Here, Caprioli, Bull and the other captains were in conference.

"Somebody holed the ships from the inside", they heard the grim voice of Opzoom. "We can only hope that they touch bottom before they fill up completely."

"And how do you plan to get to the leaks? We are not fish, you know!" growled Bull viciously.

"Count, we can save the ships" Bilg shouted, "they have secret hatches! We will show them to you – but we need a couple of strong men with heavy hammers to close them!"

Such hatches were unknown on ordinary ships, that's why the captains couldn't understand this.

"Nonsense!" growled Bull and Opzoom only had a dismissive hand gesture. Caprioli, however understood immediately, that Larissa and Bilg must be right, as it would have been impossible to hole the thick walls of the ships unnoticed. The use of these devilish hatches also became clear: they could spoil the capture of an enemy crew and yet save themselves. On their raids, they were dependent on sailors from captured ships for crew, pressed into service.

"Let's go! Let's try it!" commanded Caprioli decisively. Nieselpriem already had a heavy axe which could be used as a hammer, in his hand. The captains joined in by grabbing heavy steel poles and other useful tools, as it would have taken too long to fetch heavy hammers from below.

Caprioli, Bull and Nieselpriem jumped with Bilg unto the lowest lying "Devil"; the others hurried with Larissa to the "Death".

Indeed: they found sliding hatches on the lowest deck, the one just above the keel, on both ships – one each on the port and starboard side near the bow, and two more in the stern.

On each of the brigantines, only one hatch had been tampered with.

But, whoever had opened them was a bit too hasty or purposely wanted the ships to sink so slowly, that disaster wouldn't be discovered till nightfall, when there would be no possibility of rescue. Both on the "Devil" and the "Death", the hatches had only been opened a few inches. The entering water had already filled the large keel areas and flooded the floor of the lower deck.

The water was almost chest high, but the men still managed to shut the hatches.

If the saboteur had planned to let the ships sink at night, then he had miscalculated by opening the hatches too much.

As there now was no more danger, the prisoners had to remove the water with whatever containers were available, and form a long chain to pass these on deck and pour them over board. Every available pump was brought on board the two brigantines, where the soldiers manned them as ordered, but leisurely, leaving the heavy work to the pirates.

As emptying the ships in this manner would have taken many days, Caprioli ordered the ships carpenters to build cranes. Ropes and winches were mounted to these and the attached barrels lowered and lifted, like drawing water from a huge well.

It still took three days before the brigantines had been raised to their normal waterline position.

As soon as Caprioli had organised the lifting of the ships, changed into dry clothes and all other needed chores were under way, Larissa and Bilg told him that they had to tell him something secretly. He took them to his cabin. Now he listened to them and to his surprise, heard not only how they had discovered the secret hatches and how they had subdued the pirate, but also how they found the treasure.

"You have done fantastic work, and achieved much more than you probably realise", praised Caprioli. "Without your discovery the raised brigantines would have been lost; you have captured them again. On top of that is not only the treasure you discovered; I think that we will find similar hoards on board the other two pirate ships. I can't say much more right now, because swift action is required to avoid any more calamities, but your due share is definitely yours."

"I give my share to Bilg", Larissa said quickly "because other than tripping the pirate, I didn't do anything. Everything else Bilg did."

Bilg wanted to object, but Caprioli, smiling raised his hand and then in friendship put an arm around his shoulder

"We can discuss all that later, children, there is plenty of time. But something else can happen now. Bilg from now on you are no longer a drummer boy, but the regimental drummer.

Go to the quartermaster and tell him to give you sub lieutenant's stripes. You, my dear Larissa, I can't reward you, only your father can do that – and I am sure he will."

Bilg stood confused, with a red face and couldn't say another word. But Larissa said lightly:

"If you think that I deserve a reward, uncle Cyps, I could make a suggestion." She looked at Bilg out of the corner of her eye. "But, that we can discuss later, it also has plenty of time. By the way, you could like me as much as you do Bilg, otherwise I will be jealous, and I don't want that."

Caprioli laughed loudly, put his other arm around Larissa and pulled them both close to him.

"You are my lovely heroes, you can stay that way! But no", he corrected himself, "You are real heroes, nobody will equal that for a while!"

The sail makers on the "Fantoma" were given the job of sewing strong foot long bags, using the best sail cloth they could find on the pirate ships, and bring them to his cabin.

Then he had a confidential discussion with Nieselpriem and Borromaus the gunnery chief. He told them that the pirate's loot is probably hidden in the lower stern section of the ships and ordered them to make sure that nobody went to these areas as soon as the ships had risen enough.

He also informed gunnery chief Bichler and send him along with Larissa and Bilg to guard the treasure on board the "Hell".

As soon as the first ten bags were finished, Caprioli along with Habakuk, who carried the bags, went to the "Hell".

"Wow that must be the treasure from many years! Caprioli exclaimed, as he looked inside the barrel found by Larissa and Bilg. "It will be a hard task to divide all this stuff rightfully."

Habakuk now had to fill and then tie the bags well. Then he hefted one across his mighty neck and two under each arm and returned to the "Fantoma" with Bilg.

In this manner the moor carried all the gold to Caprioli's cabin. Bilg remained to guard the treasure.

"The tied up pirate is still there!" remembered Larissa.

"Yes, right, we almost forget him!" laughed Caprioli.

When Habakuk returned, he had to untangle him from the net and stand him on his feet. Habakuk had his own way of dealing with characters like that. He pinched his rear end with his steel like fingers and the pirate, with a loud scream, was instantly amenable.

"I many more jokes know", said Habakuk with a friendly smile. "If count ask and you not answer or lie, I completely eat you. You sure taste good!"

In reply, only a gurgling sound escaped the pirate's throat. But when Caprioli began to question him, the answers flew out in a rush. If he couldn't find an answer right away, then all it took was for Habakuk to show him his teeth or approach his rear end a bit, and he talked again like a wound up clock. So it came out that he was the oldest of the three pirate brothers and their leader. He was the one who captured the "Vlissingen" and had planned to keep its gold treasure for himself.

The man was put in chains with extra care and imprisoned in an empty chamber on the "Fantoma".

The heavy and secretive bags that Habakuk had carried from the "Hell" to the "Fantoma" and the odd arrangements that Caprioli had made for the brigantines, had stirred up the curiosity and suspicion of the captains and crew.

At their request Bull and Opzoom, with stern faces, went to see Caprioli. The white bearded Dutchman asked:

"With your permission, we are curious as to what is going on here, count. What is in the bags that your servant carried to your cabin, and what is the meaning of the guards on the brigantines? If you don't mind me asking!"

A dangerous glimmer appeared in Caprioli's eyes. Playfully he swung his monocle on its fine gold chain around his finger.

"Yes, I do mind you asking, especially you. Here you are only a captain without a ship, a captain we rescued. I am the military commander of this fleet! Think about that when you speak to me!" The count's voice was as sharp as the sabre at his side. "I regret to have to speak to you like that, captain Opzoom, but if one does not understand to stay within the boundaries of required respect, than he has to be reminded. I will however willingly tell you what is in the bags my servant carried: first, the gold from the "Vlissingen"."

"My gold!" groaned Opzoom, "the company's gold!"

"That *was* your gold or the company's, captain!" Caprioli made it clear. "The pirates robbed you of the gold, when your ship was misguided by false lights and went aground on this island. That we learned from the pirate chief himself. And then, the gold was recovered twice by others: the first time, when the crew of the "Fantoma" overpowered the gang on board the "Hell" and captured her. And the second time, when young Bilg and the lady Larissa found the gold and with their bravery and alertness saved the three brigantines and their treasures from sinking. And, by the way, you received as gift from Captain Bull, the exact amount that was entrusted to you by the gentlemen in Amsterdam. One ducat is as good as the next, and no one will know where they came from when you deliver them; they are all good Dutch ducats from the same mint. And now, be quiet", he added angrily, as Opzoom wanted to answer, "Don't lose my respect for you by saying that Bull's gift is one thing and the company's rescued ducats are something else!"

"But why do you trust the gunnery chiefs more than us captains, not to mention Nieselpriem?" growled Bull.

"To the best of my knowledge, the captain's main responsibility is to supervise the work of their crews", answered Caprioli seriously. "In future, it would be more beneficial for you, to think about the gold that is rightfully yours. And now, enough talk: I herewith give you my order, Captain Bull and you captain Opzoom that you will tell the other captains, that under the supervision of trustworthy witnesses, the gold will be brought on board the "Fantoma". There, it will stay under my care for the time being.

The captains are to tell the crews, that all will receive their fare share, no matter what rank or station. What the shares will amount to will be determined once all the gold is safely stored together. I will talk to my soldiers personally."

Caprioli turned and walked off without another word.

The two captains walked off like wet poodles.

TO EACH HIS OWN

There was happy and noisy jubilation on board the ships, after Caprioli had spoken with his soldiers and the captains with their crews. Caprioli had to hide in his cabin from all stormy gratitude from the men.

The preparation of the ships was completed in no time. The pirates atoned for most of their life's sins with the help of a few curses, balled fists and kicks from the sailors and soldiers. From the on the "Hell" imprisoned pirate chief and with Habakuk's friendly help, Caprioli quickly found out who the third pirate brother was: the one that had been beaten by Larissa's swordplay! And when Caprioli offered them to the teeth gnashing moor for breakfast, they found no problem to tell them where the rest of the hidden treasures where. These two had also used the stern section of their ships as treasure chests. One had hidden it in a large stack of powder kegs. The other one, the most successful one, had filled a gigantic oak chest with the robbed gold. But under that chest, Larissa and Bilg discovered a hidden trap door. A steep ladder led to a room, where on other ships the spare anchor chains were kept. The robber had collected a mountain of gold, the height of a man, there. A skeleton was lying on top of the gold, clothed in mouldy, torn rags. Was it to be a warning or deterrent, or was it a thief who got trapped there...?

Habakuk stacked more than five hundred bags of gold in his master's cabin as well as two adjoining chambers. A sheer immeasurable treasure!

The treasure was secure, the ships lay at anchor ready for sea, and nothing stood in the way of departure. Before setting sail, Caprioli gathered all the captains, the officers he had promoted to captain the pirate ships and a delegation of sailors and soldiers.

"Comrades" he said to them, "it is impossible to work out the value of the treasure and to pay out the shares before the end of this journey. But everyone who has been part of this voyage to now, whether they wear skirts or pants has been in great danger. Every one therefore should have a part of the loot. Take it as a down payment of the full share that will be paid out to you in Paramaribo. My estimate of the treasure is so vast, that everyone can have thirty ducats right away. My loyal servant Pelegrin will prepare the shares for each crew and hand them to their captain. The gunnery chiefs will get the share for the soldiers. The rest of the bags will be sealed in your presence; every seal will be stamped with the coat of arms on my ring. Start, Pelegrin!"

Soon, the gold pieces jingled on the large table in Caprioli's cabin. Pelegrin carefully wrote out the list of names and Borromaus counted out the sparkling ducats.

Caprioli watched for a while and then turned to Larissa.

"Please go and get your Baba", he asked her, "and you Bilg, accompany Larissa."

The two looked surprised at each other, but did as they were told without a word.

As black Baba entered, she screamed in delight when she saw the mountain of gold.

Caprioli placed his hand on Borromaus' arm:

"Now push five times thirty ducats to me", he said with an impish smile.

He placed the first pile in Baba's hands.

"Because you saved your mistress from the two pirates!"

"Oh, I not rescue mistress", she protested and pressed the hand with the ducats protectively to her bosom. "Mistress, protect herself, she shoot and stab like real pirate!"

"I believe that completely, Baba", Caprioli, replied laughing "she has already given us a demonstration!"

"I put all pirates in wash tub, and Habakuk too", she confirmed with rolling eyes and glittering teeth.

Habakuk grinned and gave her a slap on the rear end. But she wasn't mad.

The second pile, Caprioli placed in Larissa's hands.

"Oh, uncle Cyps", she said, "That is the first money I earned myself!" She pushed it to Bilg. "There, look after it fore...look after it please."

Undecided, Bilg looked from Larissa to Caprioli and hesitantly tied it in his handkerchief.

Now Bilg received his share. With sparkling eyes he stuffed the ducats in his pockets.

"And what will you do with your riches?" Caprioli asked him.

"I will buy my own compass; sea charts and books from far away countries."

The count gave him a scrutinising look:

"So, you really want to become a seaman?"

Bilg, nodded with enthusiasm.

"Maybe, one day, I'll capture my own booty; then I'll buy my own ship and become my own captain!"

Pelegrin pushed his ducats carelessly aside. Habakuk also did not want to accept them at first. But, then he did take them, and gave them grinning to Baba. She took the gold, beamed like a hall full of lit candles and winked at Habakuk, before returning to her chores.

Finally, everyone had received their share, and Pelegrin started counting the rest of the loot before sealing it in the bags. He pressed Caprioli's ring into the soft wax of each individual seal. When the last of the seals dangled on the cord closing its bag, Caprioli took back his ring and occupied himself with the captains, sailors and soldiers.

"The job would only be half done if I kept the ring, as I could secretly open the bags and then replace the seal. That is why one of you should have it and carefully guard it, until we arrive in Paramaribo.

He studied the faces row by row.

"There, you take it and show it to your fellow crew members" he said to one of the sailors, that served on the "Fantoma". "Do you want to...?"

The man took the ring hesitantly with an embarrassed smile and shoved it in his pocket.

The captains had silly looks on their faces, because the count had not entrusted the precious ring to one of them.

"The hardest part of this voyage still lays ahead of us, gentlemen", he said to them, "I cannot lead a fleet with five hundred soldiers who are at sea for the first time and eight competent captains a. But with two hundred well meaning seamen and a bit of luck, eight good captains could safely deliver the fleet to Paramaribo. The cargo that the "Fantoma" now carries is far more dangerous than a full cargo of gun powder. I hope we understand each other!"

The captains saluted and left.

"Phew!" said Caprioli, "that's done. However: I don't feel comfortable about this affair. I would prefer a cargo of rocks."

Pelegrin smiled quietly to himself.

"You know these people, count", he said. "You negotiated well with them!"

"To live and let live, and not to confuse the written law with the righteousness of the heart, that is the whole secret, my friend", answered Caprioli.

THE SEAHORSES

The frigates and brigantines sailed out of the bay, with a sparkling sun rising on the horizon. One after the other they dove into the veil of the early morning fog and disappeared like ghost ships.

The sailors and soldiers went about their work with laughter and enthusiasm. All felt themselves under the protection of the wonderful count and new that their share of the booty was safe. Many an old sea dog saw himself, as a well off man, relaxing in a rocking chair for the rest of his life. Others wanted to build a house and raise a family, and others again, dreamed of a boat, with which they could go out fishing on their own account.

The fleet sailed a keel line well spaced apart. In the lead was the "Fantoma" again. The wind was good and steady, and appeared to promise a fast voyage.

Caprioli stood in the bow of his ship, and searched the sea with his spyglass, over and over again, but, each time, disappointed handed it back to Pelegrin. Other than the odd seagull swaying on the waves, their seemed to be nothing to discover on the long and even swells of the Atlantic,

An unfamiliar sound made him look up.

Pelegrin also became attentive.

"A horse neighed, count..." he said with a voice that betrayed that he didn't believe his own ears.

Caprioli laughed.

"What else should a horse do, I've never heard a horse sing!"

Pelegrin became angry.

"You are joking, count, horses don't neigh in the ocean!"

"Why not? If there are horses in the ocean, then they will neigh in the ocean."

The old man sighed; it was again impossible to have a sensible discussion with the count today.

He followed Caprioli to the rail.

Close to the hull of the ship swam a large stallion and two mares.

They looked up with longing eyes, and neighed quietly at Caprioli.

"Veritable horses – real horses!" marvelled Pelegrin. "It seems you didn't dream after all when you told me about your ocean voyage on the stallion!"

Caprioli, smiling, shrugged his shoulders, reached in his pocket and pulled out a handful of sugar cubes. He threw one to the stallion. Skilfully, the stallion caught it and licked his pink mouth. The anxious mares also received their share.

In the meanwhile, the whole ships company became aware of the strange water animals; everybody wanted to see the horses. Captain Bull couldn't get them back to work, no matter how much he cursed.

"I want the horses to get used to the ship and try and tame them", Caprioli said to Bull, "Because no king has such animals in his stable. Can you get a large area cleared on the fore deck?"

"How do you plan to catch these weird animals, and with what will you feed them, if you really catch them? You can't build a stable here!" growled the captain.

"Let that be my concern, Bull, the animals won't disturb you."

Unwilling, Bull gave the necessary orders, and soon the fore deck was as bare as a dance floor.

Caprioli, who had continued to feed the animals with sugar cubes, clicked his tongue invitingly and stepped back from the rail. He wasn't mistaken: The water along the top sides whooshed, with a powerful kick the stallion lifted itself from the water, over the rail and landed softly on deck next to Caprioli. Seconds later the two mares followed. Begging, the beautiful animals pushed at Caprioli with their velvety snouts. They competed for attention, as his hand continuously reached in his pocket and pushed the sweet sugar cubes between their lips.

Sailors and soldiers forgot about their work in astonishment over the huge sinewy horses, with their green eyes, undulating manes and their long tails that reached to the floor. Even Captain Bull and coxswain Nieselpriem, watched the enticing game, and were so captivated, that they forgot to order the men to work.

Most surprising was the fact that they had hooves, but they were so soft, that their movements and little jumps, were almost inaudible.

One of the sailors had called Larissa. She came running with Bilg, but stopped surprised, some distance away. Neither she, nor her companion could understand where these horses, with which Caprioli intimately played, came from. She quickly regained her practical thinking ability, and came to terms with the surprising reality. She was used to horses since childhood, and since their departure, secretly looked forward to some wild riding in Paramaribo. She had never seen beautiful animals like these. She asked Bilg to get a small bag of ships rusks. When he came back with it, the two of them stood next to Caprioli. Larissa, with a rusk on her flat hand, reached out towards one of the mares. The animal looked at her with shining eyes, sniffed the rusk, carefully took it with her lips and started to chew. The mare liked the unfamiliar thing and pushed Larissa hand begging for more. Larissa gave her another piece.

Now the other mare and the stallion became curious and snuggled up to Larissa.

Caprioli, whose pockets were now empty, watched with a smile.

Now Bilg took a piece of rusk and offered it to the stallion. The stallion snorted, and as he carefully took it, Bilg, gently stroked his soft snout. He did this with such experience and as a matter of course, that Caprioli was surprised. Larissa knew how to handle horses, Caprioli knew that. But this boy ...?

"Have you had something to do with horses before, as you are not afraid at all?" Caprioli asked him.

"Oh, yes, earlier on, count", was his monosyllabic answer.

Caprioli didn't want to push him anymore. In his mind however, he planned to pay more attention to this strangely attractive boy. Ships boys often had mysterious fates, before they signed on when they arrived in a strange port. Captains never asked many questions, as they were happy when a strong and strapping young man, signed on for one of the hardest of all jobs. This Bilg was no ordinary lout, who ran away from a poor family home; otherwise, for example, he wouldn't have understood how to get along so well with the very demanding Larissa. There was a secret about this boy, and Caprioli was determined to find out what it was.

Now, the rusks were finished too, and the horses realised that there was nothing left to nibble on. The mare that Larissa had fed first, made one last try. She sniffed Larissa's face and nibbled her ear with soft lips. The girl took her head and gave her a kiss on the nostrils.

"It seems you quickly became friends", said Caprioli laughing.

"I hope so, uncle Cyps; horses are as wonderful as dogs!"

The stallion reared neighing, and with a great leap, jumped back in the water. The mares followed him.

"Oh, too bad!" cried Larissa, "I really believed they would stay!"

"They are seahorses Larissa" Caprioli, reminded her. "It's a miracle that they came on board at all."

"They will come back", Bilg consoled her, "I saw it in their eyes!"

BILG BECOMES CAPTAIN'S APPRENTICE AND PLAYS GHOST

Since their departure from the pirate's island, Bilg no longer lived in the dark corner deep under the gun deck. As regimental drummer he wasn't entitled to an officer's cabin yet, but Caprioli made a decree. Even captain Bull didn't object to this decree, as the once cabin boy, had him worried for some time now. Although Bilg always completed the chores he was given, willingly and well, but something in his nature, did not fit the pattern of the usual cabin boy. Although, begrudgingly, he agreed that Bilg was sent to the bridge a number of hours a day, and was taught by Nieselpriem, the many faceted art of navigating a ship. But when the coxswain started to teach him things a captain needs to know, for example, the science of getting a ship's position by the sun and stars, he had enough.

He accosted Nieselpriem, and told him to concern himself with his own business, and not to tell the young boy, things that he – Nieselpriem had only read in fairy tales. It didn't help much that the coxswain loudly protested against such insults. Bull, only became angrier, took the boy aside and started teaching him everything that the captain of a big ship needs to know. He even gave him some tips that experienced captains keep secret from each other. Nieselpriem could not offer Bilg such knowledge. Bull, stroked his beard, satisfied to see his coxswain behind the tiller, starring wistfully and ashamed at the sea ahead. Naturally, he did not suspect, that Nieselpriem, when off watch, grinning, told the count how he had coerced the captain into teaching Bilg all the intricacies of seamanship. After all, it wasn't necessary that the captain knew everything, because he already was so incredibly smart.

The crew quickly got used to seeing Bilg on the bridge, instructed in the art of steering the ship by Nieselpriem and other seafaring tricks by the captain. The sailors were happy that Caprioli had chosen one of them to someday become a coxswain, or maybe even a captain. So, they were not surprised when Caprioli had the rope and candle chamber, which was close to his own cabin, emptied and rebuilt as living and sleeping quarters for Bilg.

Bilg took this surprising change calmly. To him, it was natural, to rise from lowly cabin boy, to drummer boy and even to regimental drummer in a few short weeks, and now, to spend most of his time, in the most holy place on the ship, the command bridge.

Shortly after Bilg had moved into his new lodging, he had a strange experience one evening. He heard a low conversation between three sailors, through the paper thin wooden wall, separating him from the crew quarters.

"Show us the ring Jaap, it's supposed to have a diamond as big as a walnut in the centre", said one. The one who was called Jaap answered:"It doesn't have any stone, it's solid gold, as you know very well, you've seen it often enough on the count, Kees."

"Na, I did not", said Kees, "I didn't look at the dandy's hands."

"You can show it to us anyway, your count-ring", the mocking voice of the third said, "We want to see something so fantastic a bit closer."

"It's staying where it is, Knueddel, you know precisely why the count gave it to me", answered Jaap defiantly.

"Don't pretend to be so high and mighty, Jaap", the voice of Kees, said, "your no angel. You can leave it in your pocket, we really just wanted to do a bit of business, the three of us, you know..."

"What sort of business...?"

Kees hesitated a bit, and said thoughtfully:

"Knueddel knows about locks from before – from a long time ago, you know."

"What does that have to do with the ring?"

"Well, my boy", Kees explained slowly, "there exist a locked door on this ship, and behind that door there is a large pile of bags. So, we thought that one could empty one, or maybe even two – we are very modest – and then fill them with pebbles. We could then replace the seal with your ring and nobody will know the difference."

"Yes, and then...?" Jaap's voice was hoarse with excitement.

"Blast, you're even more stupid than the captain allows!" Bickered Knuedel's voice, "We will share, and we won't have to say thank you for the pittance they will throw at our feet at the end of the trip."

"And when the swindle is discovered...?"

"Then we will have our proper share safely tucked away, and the count with his captains, will try in vain, to find out, who transformed the ducats into pebbles", explained Kees.

"He won't have to search for long, you creep, because he knows that he gave the ring to me!"

"So, you call me a creep, we will have to talk to you differently!" screamed Kees.

Crashing, a chair fell over. Jaap's scream stopped with a groan. A thump and the sound of a heavy fall penetrated the wooden wall.

For moments it was still.

Then Knueddel said quietly:

"Look in his pockets, but don't make any more noise, the others aren't deaf either!"

"Got it!" Kees whispered back. "And what do we do with this one now...?"

Bilg had listened to the conversation sitting up straight on his bunk. His forehead was covered in cold sweat. He was thinking feverishly; could he rescue the sailor Jaap and the precious ring on his own from the hands of these murderers? But then, it came over him like a strange power. He jumped from the bed, pulled the sheet over his head, charged out into the hall way, ripped open the door of the cabin next to him, and stepped into the room, which, was only lit by a small candle, with a terrible and frightening scream.

"The ship's kobold!" screeched Kees. His knife, with which he was about to stab the lifeless form of Jaap lying on the table, embedded itself in the table almost to the hilt. As if the devil himself was after him he crawled under the bunk.

Knueddel, rushed past Bilg out into the passage way.

Bilg looked around; Jaap, only seemed to be dazed from a hit. But there on the floor, directly in front of him, lay the dull shimmering ring.

He picked it up and walked out backwards from the cabin.

"Keep the ring, and do what the others had planned, yourself!" He heard an inner voice saying and was horrified. Disgusted, he spit.

In the almost completely dark passage way, he collided with Habakuk. The moor had been sent out to check on the commotion by his master. The surprised Habakuk grabbed Bilg with his huge fists and carried the struggling and screeching bundle, to the count's cabin. Only here, he discovered his error and almost fell on his knees before Bilg. But, Bilg didn't give him time. Breathless he told the count what had happened and returned the ring to him.

It seemed, like a dark shadow had fallen over the count's normally cheerful face.

"One of the characters is still in the cabin, you say?" he asked Bilg in an unheard off voice.

Bilg nodded "He hid under the left bunk."

"Habakuk, drag him out and tie him up", ordered Caprioli, "but let him lay where he is. And bring the knocked out sailor carefully here." He turned to Pelegrin: "And you please go directly to captain Bull, tell him what happened, and tell him to put the sailor Knueddel in irons.

Then he can come and see me.

Habakuk went smiling into the sailor's cabin and without effort, pulled the shivering sailor by one leg, from under the bunk. When he tried to bite, the moor gave him such a hook to the chin, that, he passed out through a cloud of stars. What was left of the character, he tied into a neat bundle with bits of rope that were lying around. Then he loaded the unconscious Jaap on his shoulder, carried him to the count's cabin, and carefully placed him on a couch. A shot of brandy brought Jaap back to consciousness; He hadn't suffered any serious damage.

Knueddel was quickly found. With his companion, Kees, he was put into irons, and imprisoned in a safe room.

Captain Bull let Bilg retell the whole story in Caprioli's presence. Pale with anger that, something like this could have happened on his ship he listened with clenched lips.

He didn't even laugh when Bilg told him how he had frightened the two characters.

"That is murder, count", he growled, "murder on my ship!"

"Almost murder, captain", answered Caprioli with a look. "The two will get their punishment in Paramaribo."

"As we are not at war, and war like rules don't apply, in which everyone would be under the rules of war, my people are under the law of the sea, exactly like this boy then" – pointing at Bilg - "when I transferred him to you."

"So..."said Caprioli playing with his monocle, "but if you want to judge, than think about the fact that there isn't only the written law, which does not allow anybody to take someone's life if not in fear of their own!"

Bull murmured something unintelligibly in his beard, and left the cabin with a whispered greeting.

The next morning, Caprioli climbed up to the command bridge, watched for a while how Bilg turned the wheel under Nieselpriem's supervision, and then said to Bull:

"Are you aware that the two prisoners from yesterday could be hungry...?"

A grim smile crossed the captain's face.

"They aren't hungry any more", he answered.

Caprioli flared up.

"What did you do with them?"

"Only what is normally done amongst seaman when no other treatment is used. We unchained them, tied a line under their arms, so they wouldn't drown, and towed them behind us for a little while. The rest we left to the one up there", Bull pointed at the heavens with his thick fingers, "but I think that the devil was already waiting for them. When, after a few minutes, we wanted to pull them up again, the lines were empty, cleanly bitten through, count. The devil must have teeth like razor blades…!"

"Too bad I didn't think about that when, some time ago, Habakuk and I were swept into the water amongst the dolphins and sharks, and you pretended to try and save us."

The captain balled his fists behind his back.

"You have no grounds to say that, count, you can't prove anything."

"I can't prove it to you, captain. But, if I could have proven it to you, I would have been a better judge."

"An eye for an eye, a tooth for a tooth!" grated Bull.

"Should I remember this saying for you, captain?" Caprioli asked quietly. He didn't wait for an answer, nodded at Bilg and descended back on deck.

The captain was right: the law of the sea was the sailor's law, and he would have no power over them if he did not follow it. Besides that, he knew that a man's life, especially on a ship, was only worth as much as it's useful. If it became unfit or even dangerous, then the judge becomes a terrible avenger.

THIRST

Two weeks had passed since the murder attempt, and the sad end of the two criminals.

Since then Habakuk carried the ring on a thin gold chain, visible to everyone, around his neck. No one dared to make a criminal suggestion, nor even think about taking the ring from him, and everyone believed in his honesty as much as that of the count.

The three wonderful sea horses appeared a number of times on deck. Because Caprioli had organised a comfortable and soft camp, made from dried sea weed, for them, the lay there for hours and let themselves be spoiled by Caprioli, Larissa, Bilg and even Habakuk. They even tolerated Pelegrin. However, should anyone else try to come close to them, the stallion would jump up snorting, and wave his fore legs at them threateningly.

They also got names in the meanwhile, and if called they would point their ears and come.

Caprioli had named the stallion "Schilg", and one of the mares got the name "Schnalge". Larissa had asked to be allowed to find a name for the mare that was particularly friendly to her. For days she pondered, trying to find a special name. Finally she found one: from now on the mare was called "Sala".

So now, all three horses had names that were as strange as they were.

The old horseman, Caprioli, made an interesting discovery: The soft hooves of the animals became firmer day by day. At the beginning he had hoped to tame them and make them into extraordinary riding horses. When he had first seen their soft hooves he had with sadness, given up the idea, as they would never be able to gallop on the hard ground. Now, he was hopeful to achieve his goal after all.

A great worry occupied Caprioli's and his captains minds, as much amusement as the horses brought to the monotone ships life, Since the fleet had passed through the mysterious Sargasso Sea, and left the many islands of intertwined sea weed behind, the wind had stopped. The sea was still, like pale shining lead in a melting pot. The ships sat without movement with hanging motionless sails. Above all that was the shimmering heat of the sun.

As the fleet should have arrived in Paramaribo some time ago, only a few of the barrels in the ships hold, still had small amounts of warm and foul water left in them. The last of the fresh food supplies, which had been taken on this long journey, because of the humid heat, lay rotten in the hold. The salted pork was inedible, because it would make one's thirst unbearable. Also the hard ships biscuits would cut the sensitive mouths without a drink.

Larissa, whose laughter would normally ring through the ship like church bells, lay most of the day, exhausted from the heat and thirst, in her cabin; she was so weak that she could barely move. Baba moved gloomily around, and Bilg used the last of his strength to stay on his feet. Pelegrin and Habakuk were only shadows of themselves. The only one who from the outside, appeared normal and unaffected by the heat or thirst, was Caprioli. Only his tall frame wasn't as upright as before and the skin of his face and hands began to take on the colour of old tobacco leaves more and more.

The captains, sailors and soldiers, started to lose hope of ever seeing their homeland again. The part of the crew that wasn't feverish or completely exhausted, sat silently brooding in whatever shady corner they could find. Longing, they waited for the tiniest breath of wind.

The blue bodies of sharks cruised in ever smaller circles around the ships. Every once in a while there was sudden excitement and for a few seconds the water foamed and turned red: Again, one of the crew, confused by fever and thirst, had fallen into the sea.

On one of these terrible days, Caprioli walked with a lantern, along the row of water barrels to inspect them. He tapped each one, but most of them sounded empty. One, by the sound of his tapping, told him that it still held some water and he tried a little taste. The warm and foul liquid couldn't do anything for his thirst.

"Well, how do you like this, honourable count?" he suddenly heard Scheitanoff's familiar voice, penetrate his thoughts.

Untouchable, in a pale green light, he stood next to Caprioli. The count could see the barrels through his body.

"Even though we are not allowed to touch the likes of you or have the right to wring your neck, we have other things that can work for us", his Excellency continued. "Sharks don't always let themselves be ridden, octopuses don't always commit suicide, lightning bolts are not always available to melt cannons in the last minute; and it's not always possible to freeze a polar bear's paws. Oh, I have patience honourable count, lots of patience – and many more possibilities to persuade you to do a little business with me."

Caprioli remained silent. Slowly, moving forward, he continued tapping the barrels.

"Till now, you only had luck, lots of luck", hissed Scheitanoff, "but now luck will not help you!" He pointed at the empty barrels and laughed spitefully. "No clever idea or unusual coincidence will make it possible for you to fill these barrels with water. And your Pelegrin won't have a chance to enter this last of your adventures into his diary, unless – you join this group. "From one of his coat pockets, he pulled out a roll of parchments and extended a sheet with neatly pre written text to the count.

"You know we stayed very old fashioned and can't do it any other way", he continued his flattering excuse, "we still use the old favoured method: just a little signature at the bottom of an honest contract and – believe me – you will have found a friend, better than you'll ever find!"

He looked at Caprioli with his shark's eyes with the look of an innocent angel and offered him a pen. "Just a tiny drop of blood on the pen and your signature will seal our contract."

Because Caprioli still ignored him, he continued: If this method is too silly for you, dear count, it is sufficient if you just sign in thought. Most nobles did it that way in the last hundred years..."

The count stopped and looked at the infernal excellence with narrowed eyes.

"Do you also have Captain Bull's contract there?" he asked incidentally.

"Captain Bull...? That contract got lost so to say, and not without your fault as you well know. You still owe me a replacement for that loss!"

Caprioli continued walking.

Scheitanoff waddled behind him on flat feet and eagerly talked at him:

"Wait dear count, I am paying you a price that you can name yourself, for your signature. And what am I paying for? For nothing, if you think about it seriously. What I want to buy, you can't see nor touch, it is less than air, and most people say that it does not even exist."

Again he extended the parchment and the pen to him.

"Sign dear count, at least in thought, you will lead a happy life, and you will never see me again if you don't want. At least for now", he added carefully.

Caprioli silently tapped the next barrel.

Scheitanoff beseeched him:

"You have no other way now to save yourself and the people on the ships. Think about the poor women, your god daughter!"

Pleading, he raised his hands.

"Do you want to murder them or me...? Caprioli asked drily.

"I...?" Scheitanoff pretended to be surprised.

"I only want to help you and all the others, for a laughably small deal! Can you blame me for that? You too make your deals, count!"

Caprioli did not reply.

Scheitanoff tried again.

"If you sign, I will instantly fill every barrel with cool, clear spring water!"

"Don't try so hard Scheitanoff; what you want does not have a price, no price at all. You are crazy, and at the moment the people think am crazy, that is one of the differences between us."

Lurking, Scheitanoff asked:

"Don't you think at all, about what the gentlemen in Amsterdam will say about you, when the famous Caprioli arrives with a death fleet in Paramaribo, or maybe takes the whole fleet to hell...?"

"Give yourself the answer", replied Caprioli, while tapping the last barrel. "It is only good that every devil has to buy what he wants to own. To buy, one needs someone to sell."

"How right you are, count, here money and here the goods. You are the commander of this fleet, the leader of all these people. Does not the honour, of the highest ranking officer, demand a sacrifice for those under his protection, if one could even call it a sacrifice?"

"Honour demands not to speak with you. You reminded me of honour. Good, you have heard my last word."

Scheitanoff disappeared like the flame of a blown out candle.

The ships cat hissed at the count from the top of a barrel.

HOPE AND...

Driven by an unexplainable unrest, Caprioli went back up on deck.

Again he looked at the sky and the sea, in hope to discover a sign that a wind would come up, and with it a rescue. But, like for days now, the cloudless sky glowed in a pale blue. The endless surface of the sea stretched out like a slippery mirror and disappeared in the haze of the horizon.

Captain Bull approached the count. The mighty body of the old seaman, hung like his own ghost in his clothes. His eyes were like small dying fires, in a withered face.

"It is the end count", he croaked with a voice that sounded like a rusty door hinge. "It is my fault, my fault alone, because I smuggled that devil Scheitanoff on the ship. You will see, when the sharks get me, this devilry will disappear and the wind will start blowing."

"Don't talk gibberish, Bull!" prevailed Caprioli, "that character would have been on board without your stupidity. I have not been to any place in the world without meeting him."

The captain pointed at the deck planks.

"There, see yourself that there is no hope left, even if wind and rain would put out this glowing hell. The planks warped and cracked in this hellish heat. The water is rising in the keel; the ships could spring a leak any moment, and I don't have any men to man the pumps. And look up there at the sails! They are scorched and will rip like tinder at the first puff of wind. It wouldn't surprise me, if they didn't burst into flames on their own soon. Say what you wish count, but here your wisdom is at an end, just like your luck!"

Gunnery chief Borromaus, who had heard the last few words, came hobbling on his wooden leg. His face, unshaven for days, was covered with a long white beard. The tips of his moustache hopelessly drooped down.

"That is also my opinion count", he said with a toneless voice. "My powder kegs could burst into flame any minute. If I had them cooled with sea water, then the powered could get wet and we would be defenceless."

"I know all that myself", answered Caprioli, "but do you know the story of the two frogs that fell into a milk jug?"

"I am not in the mood for jokes or funny stories, count", growled Bull, and Borromaus thought that the count shouldn't conjure up more disasters with light hearted jokes.

"Listen to this little story anyway", answered Caprioli, "maybe it will become clear to you then, why I never lose my courage. So, the two frogs swam around in the milk, despaired. Their situation was hopeless, as bad as a hopeless situation can be, because the smooth walls of the jug didn't give them the slightest foothold, to climb out. One of the frogs, who thought himself as the most sensible, stopped swimming after a while, sank and drowned. The other one kept on swimming. Suddenly he felt solid ground under his feet. He couldn't understand where it came from, but kept kicking undaunted. Suddenly he sat on a large piece of butter, which had formed through his kicking. With one jump, he hoped onto the edge of the jug, and there to freedom."

"I would rather sit in a cool jug of milk and drown, than here in this hell and roast alive", screeched Bull. "Do you expect me to laugh at this simple minded story, count"

"I am not laughing either Bull, but I understood this story", countered Borromaus. "I am not giving up either, so there!"

The captain pointed at his forehead, and toddled off like a wounded bull.

Following a sudden idea, the gunnery chief also hobbled off. He gathered a few soldiers, who could still stand on their feet, covered the powder kegs with tar smeared sails and poured streams of sea water over them. This way, the powder was cooled down without getting wet.

"The sea horses are playing outside again", said Bilg to Caprioli.

"I wonder what they drink. Not the salty sea water."

The count looked at Bilg thoughtfully and walked to the railing with him.

"Look, Bilg, what does the mare "Sala" have in her mouth?" Caprioli asked in surprise.

"I don't know count, something odd anyway."

Caprioli whistled, clicked his tongue and called the mare by name. Immediately she swam along, jumped on deck and placed the thing at his feet like a well trained dog. It looked like a gourd with a long, smooth stem. No doubt, it was a fresh fruit which grew on one of the plants in the huge sea weed forests in the Sargasso Sea.

"Take your knife and cut off the top end with the stem", Caprioli told him.

The fruit was soft and easy to cut.

"Look, count, it is hollow and full of juice!"

Caprioli poured a few drops in his hand and tasted it. The juice was cool, clear and had a delicious peach taste.

Hopefully, the stuff isn't poisonous", warned Bilg.

"Sala" surely wouldn't have it in her mouth if it were poisonous", answered Caprioli. "Try it yourself."

Bilg also tasted a few drops. "Delicious!" he marvelled.

Caprioli gently stroked the mare's neck.

"Now, take the fruit to Larissa, pour the juice into two glasses and give it to her and Baba, the two are the worst off among us, I think", He ordered Bilg after a short consideration.

The mare jumped back in the water and Caprioli saw, how she and her companions dove and soon after surfaced some distance away. If the horses really drank the juice of these fruit, then one not only found the answer to the secret that Bilg had suggested, but there must be more plants in the vicinity on which they grew.

Pondering, Caprioli looked into the sea and suddenly discovered something wonderful. At about five to eight metres under the water surface, a green forest of plants stretched out before him, and in it swam thousands of these mysterious fruit. That no one had made that discovery before wasn't only due to the complete exhaustion of all the humans on these ships. During the last few days, the fleet must have been moved by an underwater current, and during the previous night, carried over the huge field of sea weed and water plants.

Caprioli's heart started beating faster when he recognised the consequences this discovery must have on all the crews and soldiers.

WONDERFUL RESCUE

When Bilg returned, he sent him to captain Bull, coxswain Nieselpriem and gunnery chief Borromaus. Disbelieving and from the weakness of their senses, barely conscious, they heard what Caprioli had to tell them. Bull again pointed at his forehead.

"I will not let you take away the last of my sanity, count", he croaked. "It would be better if you invented the ability to make wind, to escape from this witches cauldron! I have travelled the world's oceans for forty years, but I never heard of sea cucumbers filled with water."

Angry, he stomped up to the command bridge. He felt taken for a fool.

Nieselpriem longingly licked his dry lips and sank deeper within himself.

Borromaus loudly stomped the deck with his wooden leg.

"Let's try it with the help of our soldiers, if this nitwit of a captain does not want to be rescued", he said with great effort.

He attached a hook to a long rope, threw it overboard and let it sink into the plant forest. Bilg and the well refreshed Larissa went to stand next to him. With combined strength they pulled the hook up again. A thick bundle of water plants, in which hung about twenty fruit were caught in it.

"Be careful and only drink a little bit", warned Caprioli. "I don't know the effect of this juice yet, but it will surely be harmful if we pour too much into our empty stomachs."

They knelt down, cut off the tops of a few sea melons (That's what Caprioli had called them) and drank the delicious cool juice in long thirsty draughts.

"I also tried the flesh of these fruit, it tastes delicious, uncle Cyps", said Larissa. But just like a real melon, you can only eat the inside."

She cut open a fruit that had been drained of juice, and bit hungrily into its meat.

The others copied her.

Borromaus happily twirled the ends of his moustache.

"I think we are saved once more, count", he said smacking and chewing. "If you would have given up, we would have died of thirst, yet all we had to do was to stretch out our hands to have the most wonderful water in the world.

Content, he closed his right eye to a small slit.

Caprioli, after a long time, stroked his silver white goatee again.

"You did believe me, Borromaus, but still: Don't ever forget this lesson! And now to work! You, Borromaus, shoot off the bow cannon to get the attention of the other ships. Bilg will order the captains with flag signals, to man the boats and come on board the "Fantoma" for a discussion. I will get a few soldiers and sailors to fish out as many sea melons as possible. Larissa and Baba should drink their fill, and then we will help the sick and weak to get back on their feet. Don't forget the prisoners."

Thundering, cannon shot rolled over the sea.

The sailors and soldiers, of the "Fantoma", those that managed to drag themselves a few steps, went to the bow and stormed Borromaus with questions about the meaning of the cannon shot. The glowing slow match still in his hand, he told them of the count's wonderful discovery. It didn't take long before the crew, using any usable instrument, fished out mountains of sea melons and refreshed themselves. From the last ship of the fleet, the "Imago", gunnery chief Bichler, fired off a cannon shot, in reply to his comrade Borromaus. The cannon fire, livened up the crews on all the ships, and especially the captains and coxswains, who stared over at the "Fantoma". Here, Bilg was on the bow, and signalled Caprioli's command to the captains, to come on board the "Fantoma" without delay.

Habakuk, who now had quenched his thirst and had regained his deep voice, stood next to him and watched him. In his joy over the unexpected rescue, he placed the hollow of his hands around his mouth and yelled at the nearest ship:

"All captains come over, have wonderful water for all people!"

Bilg laughed at the moor's funny English, but the captain over there had understood. Although disbelieving, the order with its incredible reason was quickly passed on from ship to ship. It wasn't long, and the first boats with captains, lay alongside the "Fantoma".

"Mijnheeren, gentlemen, Senores, what I have to tell you sounds like a miracle", Caprioli started to address the assembly. "Although we did not find water, but something, that will quench a thirst even better, and on top of that, not only silences the hunger, but also makes many of our supplies palatable again."

He had Habakuk, hand him an opened sea melon and continued:

"A few metres under the water surface, you will find these unusual fruit in large quantities. Their hollow interior is filled with a delicious juice, and their flesh is tender and tastes as nice as peaches."

With a wink from Caprioli, Habakuk handed each captain and each sailor of the rowing crew a sea melon, from which he had first cut off the top.

All drank with great satisfaction, tasted the delicious flesh, and were lost for words to thank him. Finally, Caprioli showed them the boundless wealth over which the ships floated, and let the crews bring on board, masses of sea melons. Now the captains were convinced that everyone on the ships would be saved. Before the count ended the meeting, he ordered them to place tarred sail cloths in every available space, fill them with sea water, and to store an adequate supply of sea melons in them. He especially urged them to be speedy, as the ships were being pushed by a hardly noticeable current, and one could not know, when the fleet would pass the plant forest.

The captains couldn't get back to their boats and ships quick enough. Soon, one could witness from the "Fantoma" how everything came back to life on all the frigates and brigantines. In a feverish hurry, the crews fished out mountains of sea melons, and the 'hurrah' cries for the count were continues.

Captain Bull couldn't resist the temptation to secretly collect a few sea melons, greedily drink their juice and eat their tender meat. Since then, like a bad conscience impersonated, he crept near the count. One could see that he was trying to say something nice from his heart. But, Caprioli didn't even look at him. Finally, determined he approached the count and growled:

"I have to ask you for forgiveness, count, for the affair with the funny fruit before, and various other things, about which you know, but also for things that you may not be aware of. But if you are righteous – and you are righteous – then you have to admit, that it is difficult to get used to all the unusual things that happen around you."

Smiling, Caprioli played with his monocle.

"It's OK captain", he answered, "I know to appreciate your plea, and you know that I am not unforgiving. But the unusual of whom you speak, is maybe not as unusual, if one opens one's eyes. Isn't the world full of wonders?"

"And that with the lightning bolt – is that not something that goes against every reason and common sense, although I saw it with my own eyes?"

Smirking, Caprioli twirled the tips of his moustache.

"Well yes, my dear Bull", he admitted, "things like that don't happen to me either every day, but one has to understand how to handle lightning bolts!"

Bull snorted hopelessly.

"And that with the sea melons, which no seaman has ever seen before…?"

"Well, what can I say? One has to know how to find even sea melons at the right moment. That's all!"

Silently whistling, Caprioli climbed up to the command bridge to join Nieselpriem and Bilg.

Bull scratched his head and looked with open mouth at the count.

THE SEA SNAKE

The hardly noticeable current which had pushed the fleet, became a bit stronger. As there was still not a breath of wind, the ships did not respond to their rudders, and started to turn slowly around their own axis. Now, there was the danger that they would drift into side arms of the main current, and be scattered all over the ocean. If they ended up outside of visual range, they would have little chance to find their way back to the flag ship.

Caprioli stood on the command bridge with Captain Bull, Nieselpriem and Bilg. He recognised the danger, and with the dark prevision of things to come he quietly said to Bull:"I think it's time to bring the ships within towing distance from each other and tie them together; they are still close enough to row tow ropes from one to the other. What do you think?"

"Mm", growled Bull, "I thought about that some time ago, count...I just wanted to wait with this manoeuvre till you mentioned it yourself. After all, it shouldn't matter if I give the order now or later."

A smile twinkled in the corners of Caprioli's eyes and a tell-tale twitch could be seen on Bilg's mouth. Bull didn't notice. As if re evaluating a long existing thought, he rolled his lips, so that his regrown goatee stood up steeply. Then, with the countenance of a field marshal, he discussed the planed manoeuvres with Nieselpriem, and commanded him to give the required orders.

The coxswain went down on deck and climbed up the stern quarter of the "Fantoma", with a speaking tube in his hand. With a far reaching voice, he gave the order to row tow ropes from one ship to the next, to pull the ships within towing distance, and to fasten the ropes securely.

In less than an hour, the work was done.

Caprioli, carefully watched the manoeuvres, but, regularly, he looked at a particular spot in the width of the ocean.

In the last few hours, the three sea horses also seemed unusually restless. Nervously, they swam around the "Fantoma", snorting loudly, often jumping up on deck, but returned to the water immediately.

"Give me your spy glass for a moment, Bull", Caprioli, asked the captain.

Bull passed it to him.

The count looked at a particular spot in the distance for a long time, and then gave it back.

"Carefully look at that long white stripe out there, and tell me what you think about it", he told the captain.

Bull, did as he was told.

Still looking through the spy glass, after a while he said:

"It looks the current breaking on an underwater coral reef…"

Immediately looked frightened at the count.

"A reef…? In this area there are no reefs, and we barely moved a few miles in the last few weeks!"

Again, he looked intensely through the spy glass.

"That isn't a reef, count…"

"What else could it be?"

Bull wheezed.

"I am really no scaredy-cat, count, but that thing out there is very creepy!"

"Haven't you noticed that, this thing is slowly moving, that it is forming a large semi circle and approaching us with one end?"

Restless, Bull lifted the spy glass again. With big eyes, Nieselpriem and Bilg looked from the captain and then the count and back again. With bare eyes, they couldn't distinguish anything yet.

"Truly, it's alive, it moves, but it is much too long for a whale."

"Once again you are of the same opinion as I, my dear Bull", commended Caprioli. "I hope you will be of the same opinion, if I now suggest to you, to have every sail, to the last little bit of canvass, in the fleet stowed as quickly as possible."

"Stow the sails now...? The smallest breath of wind could get us under way and save us from this cauldron!"

"But, we don't have any wind, and there are no signs, that any breeze is likely to spring up, captain", Caprioli, answered him. "But if you follow my advice, we could get to Paramaribo without wind, and quicker than you could imagine."

Bull wiped his sweaty forehead with the back of his hand.

"Whoever your captain is, must come from an insane asylum, count", he groaned. "Whatever you want is contradictory, but you are always right. Why do we have our healthy common sense?"

Caprioli, smiled with a twinkle in his eyes.

"To use it properly, captain!"

"Good, I'll try, but I'll tell you this: I would rather go to hell than to do another journey with you!"

"Don't be so hasty, Bull, maybe you'll even beg me for that."

Bull snorted like a walrus. He couldn't find an answer. He grabbed the speaking tube and yelled: "Stow the sails!"

Nieselpriem also had to pass this order on to the other ships. In a few moments, the masts of the beautiful frigates and brigantines looked like trees that had been eaten bare by bugs.

Nieselpriem had taken Bull's spy glass and looked into the distance. He had barely adjusted the sights, when his knees went soft. With loose lips he stammered:"Holy Madonna, I saw a head, count, a terrible head, as big as half a house. We are doomed!"

Bilg could see it with bare eyes now.

"It's blowing water fountains in the air like a whale" he cried.

"And, what do you think that is?" said Caprioli calmly.

"Oh my God", groaned Bull, "that is an animal, a horrible animal, an animal that does not exist!"

Caprioli put his hand on Bull's shoulder.

"That's nothing more than a sea snake, and not even a very big one; it's a mile long at the most. A few million years ago, they were quite common."

"One mile...! Bull crowed. "The whole fleet is barely a mile long!"

His eyes almost pop out of his head in horror.

Calmly, Caprioli explained:

"This probably is one of the ancient animal giants that time has forgotten. In the depth of the ocean, especially around the Sargasso Sea, some of them still seem to have their hiding places. Occasionally, they are sighted by lonely sailors, but nobody believes them when they tell their story. I think this concerns another greeting from our strange gentleman, the gentleman from the "Golden Apollo" in Amsterdam, captain.

"The devil should get him!" wheezed Bull.

Caprioli, laughed. "Not a bad thought, Bull, but till now, no devil has had the idea to wring the neck of his peer. Maybe, you will talk to your friend yourself about this idea some time."

Bull, blew in his beard, and stared at the rapidly approaching monster.

Nieselpriem stared in another direction. Bilg stood fearless behind the wheel and waited for Caprioli's instructions.

"Pull yourself together, man!" Caprioli, admonished the captain. "You're shaking like jelly, and are dead before you died!"

"I have survived a few hundred hurricanes and typhoons", defended Bull, "but I don't want anything to do with sea snakes!"

"Your hurricanes and typhoons, didn't ask you whether you wanted to go for a walk with them; maybe the sea snake has no intention to attack us, maybe..."

Caprioli continue to recount his last thought. But, who knew the count, could see in his expression that an idea was developing into a solid plan.

"Come with me to the crow's nest, so we can have a better look at this creature", he told Bull. "You, Nieselpriem back to the wheel, or I'll let Borromaus shoot you into the gullet of the monster with one of his cannons. Bilg stays on the bridge to pass on commands. He should get Habakuk, to help him if needed."

From the crow's nest, one could see that monster actually was a mile long. Like a snake, it pushed itself along the water surface with slow undulations, and let itself comfortably be backed by the sun. Every once in a while it would lift its horrible head, and blow towering clouds of steam from its nostrils – and as if playing – only occupied with itself – slowly came closer. It obviously did not take any notice of the ships, which must have appeared like tiny little floating objects on the water surface. One could now clearly see with bare eyes, the monstrous, horn covered basilisk head, and the huge empty looking yellow eyes with their slit like pupils. The mouth could have accommodated a number of war ships. A thorny comb, with thick long needles, ran along the back of the animal. From time to time, the beast lifted its tail end, waved it back and forth and let it sink back into the water. A large flock of sea gulls came too close to the sea snake at the moment it inhaled. Like white smoke they disappeared in its nostrils and immediately were blown out again with a thundering sneeze.

A few large sharks, too inquisitive in their greed, swam near the head of the monster. A long, forked snakes tongue shot out and licked them up as if they were sardines.

Caprioli, thoughtful with chin in hand, observed everything with rapt attention.

"Can you be brave, captain...? He asked Bull.

The hulk might have been thinking about his adventure with the giant octopus, and answered with down turned mouth:

"Do you want me to fight that beast...?"

Caprioli smiled and shook his head.

"For the time being, it would be better to hitch the devil to his cart, instead of fighting him. It takes more than courage to do that, that's why I asked you. Look: the people on the other ships are also worried about the monster, they are waving and waiting for your orders!"

"My orders...?"

A suspicious look was directed at Caprioli.

"Have all barrels, including the water barrels sealed and thrown in the water alongside the sea snake. And, have the longest and strongest tow ropes, made ready at the bow of our ship!"

The captain looked at Caprioli with glassy eyes, swallowed and said:

"If you order it, I'll have the ship blown up under our feet to give the beast more enjoyment." He touched his head. "This is your responsibility, count!"

He took his speaking tube and yelled his orders down to the deck.

After a few minutes, the first of the barrels splashed in the water, and soon a few hundred swam in the sea.

The movement of the still distant monster, created a series of waves, and the barrels which had formed little islands, drifted slowly away from the ships.

SUPER FAST TRAVEL WITHOUT WIND

Captain Bull again stood on the command bridge. Caprioli had descended to the gun deck and was having a quiet discussion with the gunnery chief.

"It would be easier to fire off a couple of broadsides into the side of the monster", thought Borromaus. "It won't hurt us if it's dead, but then it wouldn't be useful any more either."

"The minute it is dead, it would reduce all the ships to splinters with its tail, think about it", answered Caprioli.

"If you would have told me, that you could convince the devil to say an 'Our Father', I would believe you, the way I know you now, count. But this plan..."

He stroked his white beard stubble with the back of his hand and shot a calculating look at the sea snake, less than half a mile away.

"You really want to let me down, Borromaus?"

The gunnery chief stamped with his wooden leg.

"I have never let anyone down; the one that can especially count on me is you!"

The count put a hand on his arm.

"I am happy that you are with me, Borromaus, I didn't expect anything else. But now, to work!"

The gunnery chief ordered two of the heaviest cannons, spaced three paces apart, to be mounted on the bow of the ship. A mountain of cannonballs and powder bags was placed next to the cannons.

A sailor, who had been a stonemason in the past, pierced six of the cannonballs. Long and strong tow rope ends were pulled through two lots of three cannonballs, solidly tied, and then placed into tubs filled with water.

Caprioli approached the stairs to climb up on deck again. He was called from a dark corner. With a crooked smile, Scheitanoff rubbed his hands.

"Now it's time, count", he said with a croaky voice. "A look, a small, tiny little look that betrays your quest for help and the monster out there will disappear into the depths, never to be seen again!"

Caprioli smiled rubbing his chin.

"It won't be able to dive for a while, even with your help, look for yourself, Excellency!"

He pointed at one of the wide open gun ports.

The beast, which had approached the ships, to within a few feet, smelled the barrels that at one time had been filled with fish and pickled pork. The smell made it hungry.

It opened its huge mouth a bit, and slurped up, the hundreds of barrels and head high water tubs, as if they were small morsels floating on the water.

"Not a bad idea, you could achieve high rank and recognition with us", said the surprised Scheitanoff with a devilish grin. "But this time, I planned ahead, after the barrels come the ships!"

"You don't say!"

"Will you let me help...?"

"If you have time in Paramaribo, for me to laugh at you, then you can come back, Scheitanoff. Now, I am busy!"

Caprioli turned away and climbed up on deck.

The tar smell of the ships didn't appeal to the monster. Without a care for the fleet, it slowly passed it.

Caprioli had waited for this moment. Barely four fifths of the mighty beast length had passed, when he made a sign to the gunnery chief.

Borromaus had the two heavy cannons loaded with the groups of cannonballs, to which the long tow ropes where attached. The ends of the ropes were so wet, that the short fire storm of the shots did not affect them.

The other ends of the ropes had been securely tied to the fore masts.

Once more, Borromaus, carefully aimed, then lifted his hand.

The gunner of the first cannon lowered the burning slow match to the touch hole.

The shot went off with a hissing flash and roaring thunder, whining, the tied up cannonballs followed their path, dragging the tow ropes behind them.

Seconds later, the second cannon fired.

The cannons had been aimed in such a way, that their projectiles had to land close to either side of the monster's head. But, they never touched the water surface.

The cannonballs hurtled along, the animal lifted its head listening, snapped to the left, snapped to the right, and swallowed the heavy balls like a few flies. The ropes hung out of each corner its mouth. The thundering, following the cannonballs, frightened the beast out of its comfortable peace. At first, it tried to bite through the annoying ropes. It didn't work, because they lay like bits of meat after a meal, in the gaps of its mighty teeth.

An agitated movement of its tail swept away half of the foremast and a part of the railing of the bridge.

Captain Bull and Nieselpriem flew on deck in a wide arch. Although Bull splashed into one of Baba's washing troughs, and Nieselpriem landed on a pile of dirty clothes, they didn't move any more.

Bilg stood untouched at the wheel and waved to Caprioli standing next to the bow cannons.

"That was almost a disaster", the count said to Borromaus. He ordered a sailor to look after the captain and the coxswain, put his hollow hands around his mouth and yelled up to Bilg:

"Everything on your command!"

Once more, Bilg waved with a big smile, took the speaking tube and with his high voice, yelled down to the sailors:

"Every one listen to my command!"

The sailors, still confused by the events, saluted.

Now, the monster tried to free itself with force and shot ahead as if fired from a cannon. But the ropes, stretched to the limit, held it back.

The fleet started to move. The sailors had to hurry to release enough rope, so that the tail of the beast lay just ahead of the bow of the "Fantoma".

The monster wanted to dive and flee into the depths. In the meanwhile, the mass of barrels it had swallowed, had distributed itself through its bowels, along the length of its body. The buoyancy was so great, that it swam like a cork on the surface. Again the sea snake pulled. The ropes were so stretched, that they twanged. The fleet was towed through the water at break neck speed.

Caprioli, saw the danger, beckoned Habakuk and gave him some orders.

The moor rushed off, and with the help of the sail maker Jaspers, bent a thick towing bit into a loop and spliced in five long ropes. The loose ends of the ropes were tied around the second mast and the stump of the foremast.

Habakuk, with his incredible strength, lifted the heavy loop, carried it to the bow and threw it over the thorn at the tail end of the sea snake.

Now, the beast could pull as much as it wanted, the four ropes attached to it now, wouldn't brake. It took quite some time, before the sea snake realised up front in its head that something wasn't quite right a mile back on its tail end. As it couldn't dive, it moved so fast that the empty masts of the ships bent as if a wind of hurricane strength had come up.

But the sea snake did not flee in a straight line. In wide curves, once to the left, then to the right it tried to escape and rid itself of its load.

Caprioli had counted on that.

With a chart in his hand, he climbed up to the bridge to join Bilg and set the course. Then he waved down at Borromaus.

After the count's hand signal, the chief gunnery officer aimed the cannons and lowered the slow match himself. Growling, the shot went off. The heavy cannonball, swept across the ocean in a flat curve, and landed so close to the monster's head that it grazed it, but couldn't be caught by the sea serpent.

With a frightened roar, the beast swerved. Immediately after another shot thundered. Again the cannonball hit the sea with a hiss, this time on the other side, and took a few of the horny spikes on top of the monster's head with it.

Shot after shot rolled across the ocean, until the monster, from fear, understood which direction to take, not to be bothered by more new shots.

Throughout the night, Caprioli and Bilg, who controlled the rudder masterfully, stayed up on the bridge to make sure they stayed on course. And, again and again Borromaus fired his cannon, when it was necessary to change the direction the sea serpent took. The bright light of the full moon and the green shine of the beast's body, made it easy for him to aim.

At daybreak, the South American coast emerged from the sea. When a little later, the first rays of the sun appeared, the outline of the fort at Paramaribo became clearly visible.

Now, it was high time to unload the monster, to avoid missing the saving coast.

"Cut the ropes!" Caprioli's order went from ship to ship.

The monster, suddenly freed of its burden, shot off at the speed of thought, and soon disappeared in the distant haze.

THE GREETING IN PARAMARIBO

T he ships continued their high speed passage, in spite of the continuing windless condition. Only shortly before the entrance to the harbour, did their speed reduce enough and they turned past the break water like ghost ships and dropped their anchors.

The commander of the fort and the harbour master, had observed the phantom fleet from far away with their spy glasses, and advised the governor.

At first it looked like pirates wanted to attack the city. But then, the governor recognised the flags of the Dutch-West Indies Company and the burgee of count Caprioli at the mast tops.

The governor swayed between the happiness to see Caprioli as commander of the long awaited fleet and the horror of watching the ships move at high speed in the windless conditions and without sails.

And where are the three brigantines from?

He had only been informed of five frigates!

He gave the order not to shoot, but to make every cannon of the fort ready to fire.

Although, he knew the adventures and jokes of his friend all too well – in the absence of wind, even he couldn't get a ship under way! But nevertheless...

Couldn't flags and burgees not be a treacherous disguises by the pirates? Did the devil have his hand in this game...?

Quickly he had half the troops march to the pier. The soldiers were ordered to shoot at the smallest sign of hostility.

Nothing threatening happened.

Ahead of them all, with loud cheering of her sailors and soldiers, the "Fantoma" arrived in the harbour. Anchor chains rattled, ropes were thrown on the pier, to tie up this glorious ship.

And there: amidships by the rail stood – a mistake was not possible – tall and slim, Caprioli himself, waving his hat with the famous heron feathers. On his jacket shone the diamond studded medal. Behind him, the governor recognised Habakuk and the old Pelegrin. But on the damaged command bridge, he saw a curious young man behind the wheel. He seemed to be coxswain and captain at the same time.

Then, Caprioli pulled forward, a young lady: Larissa!

Now the last doubts of the governor were gone.

Quietly he gave an order, which after surprised hesitation, was passed on to the soldiers and the commander of the fort's battery. The barrels of the cannons, high up on the walls of the fort were elevated, and as they sent their cannonballs, spewing fire and smoke, high over the fleet into the ocean, the soldiers fired off their muskets, high over the mast tops.

The unbelievable and never seen before had happened: the approaching fleet was welcomed with live ammunition!

The news of the ghost fleet spread around the little town like wild fire. The frightened people crawled into the cellars of their houses. Now however, when they heard the thunder of the cannons, the musket shots and the hurrahs of the soldiers and sailors, they streamed out to the harbour. In their enthusiasm, they could barely comprehend that the supposed pirates were actually the long awaited fleet from Amsterdam.

The last ship hadn't tied up at the pier yet, when the boarding steps rattled down from the "Fantoma", and Larissa, with flying skirts, rushed down the steps into the arms of her father.

Caprioli with Pelegrin and Habakuk, followed with measured steps to give Larissa time.

Pieter van Groenhagen, almost as tall as the count, but with full rosy cheeks and corpulent, embraced his friend.

To overcome the fright that still stayed in his bones, he called out with booming laughter:

"Ho Ho Ho, old boy, you arrive at high speed on a windless day and no sails set, as if you had the devil himself hitched up to the ships. You gave me a real fright! One of your old magic tricks again?"

Caprioli grinned.

"This time I didn't get the devil to tow the ships, but your guess still wasn't too far off."

The governor gave Pelegrin a friendly handshake, and the beaming Habakuk received tap on the shoulder.

Before boarding the carriage that was to take them to the castle, the governor took his friend aside.

"The young man I saw on the command bridge, is he the captain or the coxswain?" He asked.

"Since yesterday, he is both. The captain and the coxswain both banged their hard heads a bit, and had to stay in their bunks for the most difficult part of the trip. Now however..." He looked around and saw Bull and Nieselpriem, with sombre faces, behind the throng of pushing people. Their expressions, however brightened, when the count called them over and introduced them with words of praise. The governor's question however, was like a cold greeting.

"I heard you had an accident, captain. Despite that, will you and your coxswain be able to take command of the "Fantoma" and sail out in the morning?"

"Tomorrow morning...?

Helpless, Bull looked at the count and pointed at the badly damaged flagship.

"...with that ship...?"

Caprioli, was surprised by the question himself, but didn't say anything.

"Let me worry about the "Fantoma", captain, tomorrow morning, she will be equipped with everything necessary and ready to sail. I just want to know if you will also be ready."

"Actually, I thought that we have earned a few days of rest, Excellency", stuttered Bull.

The governor raised his eye brows.

"This, comes from a captain? The captain of the flag ship of one of the fleets of the Dutch-West Indies Company...?"

Nieselpriem wiped his nose and said hesitantly:

"The voyage was a trip through hell and now..."

"If you think you have arrived at heaven's gate, I'll slam the door to paradise in front of your nose", added the governor, laughing at the two sheepish faces. "I can see by the condition of the "Fantoma" that all kinds of things may have happened on the voyage, but the other ships seemed to have arrived safely, and the crews appear to be in good shape."

Bull blew in his beard and growled:

"Yes, Excellency, but there are a few other things to sort out…"

"Yes, very urgent things, your grace", Nieselpriem, added. With his thumb and index finger he indicated the counting of money and threw a pleading look at the count.

But the count was pre-occupied admiring the masterful architecture of the fort high above the harbour.

The governor became angry:

"Has the Dutch-West Indies Company ever owed you one single Guilder of your wages?"

Filled with indignation, Bull defended himself:

"No, Excellency, but this does not concern our wages!"

As they only had a small share in the loot, Caprioli let them stew. Only when the governor turned to him and asked:

"Can you explain to me, count, what the captain and the coxswain want?" did he answer:

"Yes, we did a bit of business along the way – I'll explain it to you later, Excellency, and those two want their share before they have to ship out again. It would be good, if you could organise a double cordon of soldiers from the "Fantoma" to a secure chamber in the castle and give Habakuk twenty strong men. They should help him to carry certain bags to security. Captain Bull and Nieselpriem will return to the "Fantoma" initially, to supervise the repairs, until your shipwright can take over. They will also organise a party of ship's officers, sailors and soldiers to oversee the transport of the bags. Pelegrin, with his list, will make sure that no bag is missing.

But first, they will deliver the governor's order to Bilg and Captain Opzoom – whom I can't see here – to immediately appear before him in the castle."

"Captain Opzoom...?" the governor asked surprised.

"Do you mean the captain of the long overdue "Vlissingen"?"

"Yes, that is the one I mean, Excellency; we fished him up on the way, as well as the most important item he was to deliver here."

The governor, uncomprehending, shook his head.

"I think you will have a lot to tell me count."

"Much more than you think, Excellency...!"

The orders for the stowage of the heavy bags were quickly carried out.

Caprioli with his friend and Larissa boarded the carriage. Surrounded by the enthusiastic cheering of the inhabitants, they ascended to the castle.

As the governor expected to have lengthy meetings, he decided to delay the welcome celebration for the dignitaries of the city as well as the officers of the garrison, the relief troops and the ship's crews, till the evening.

BIG DECISION
ARE MADE

The servant in the antechamber had to constantly remind captain Opzoom and Bilg to be patient, as the meeting between the Governor and the count seemed to go on forever. It was almost noon when they were finally allowed to enter.

Opzoom carefully sat at the very edge of the silk covered chair. Bilg sat with relaxed frankness.

"Count Caprioli told me about everything that happened on your journey" opened the governor addressing Opzoom."You lost your ship to the pirates, but you are a stout-hearted man and a good captain. The money that you were to take to Paramaribo was rescued from what I hear and ..."

Here the honest Opzoom wanted to interrupt the governor, but Caprioli gave him a meaningful look to remain quiet.

"....The Holland-West Indies Company did not suffer any losses.

Count Caprioli offered his share of the gold treasure *captured* from the pirates, as payment for the lost ship and its cargo."

"Count...!"

Opzoom looked bewildered at Caprioli.

The count raised his hand defensively.

"If this gold can help a brave and honest man it becomes honest gold. No more about this captain!"

"I will give you another command" continued the governor, "I will tell you more about this tomorrow and the count and I will discuss the proper distribution of the loot. Tell your friends and crew that this will be sorted out tomorrow as well."

Then he looked at Bilg.

"And now, to you young man. You proved on this trip that there is more in you than just a good sailor. The count has purchased an officer's commission as a reward and I commission you herewith as lieutenant. Continue to stay as modest and clean as you have been so that you can soon have your own ship as captain. A servant will take you to our scribe who will complete your officers' certificate. Now go and see our warehouse manager and get him to give you the best lieutenants' uniform in stock. If it doesn't fit, our tailor will help. This evening I want to see you dressed as lieutenant at our festive banquet."

Bilg sat pale and stiff on his chair. The governor stood up, signifying the end of the conference. Captain Opzoom had to secretly put an arm around Bilg to help him up or he would not have woken up from his enchantment.

Alone again with the governor, Caprioli withdrew a document with the emperors' seal on it from his pocket, which his friend had given him shortly after his arrival. This document had been sent with a secret messenger on a fast sailing ship. The only verbal message the courier had for the governor was an order from the emperor that Caprioli was to commence a new voyage on the morning after his arrival. Caprioli re read the document carefully.

"This will be a long and difficult voyage, Pieter. You ordered to make the "Fantoma" to be made ready for sea in the morning. I am grateful that you are offering her for my use."

The governor dismissed the thanks with a smile and a wave of his hand.

"I think that trip won't seem as long or difficult on your own ship" he added.

"On my own ship...?"

"Well yes, the "Fantoma" belongs to me, but because you returned Larissa in good health to me, I give her to you for your future voyages. You will not come across such a fine ship in the near future."

Caprioli was silent and taken aback.

It took some time before he answered thoughtfully:

"Couldn't this gift become a bit too expensive for me one day, even when you can give away a ship like a rich man can give away a gold piece?"

"There is no reason for any mistrust Cyps, I am not asking for any return service." The governor laughed.

Why shouldn't I be able to be generous to an old friend?"

"The generosity of a merchant always has a secret price, my dear Piet!"

"Aren't you the smart one?"

Pieter van Groenhagen slapped his leg with delight.

"It seems you have as high an opinion of merchants as I have of diplomats. This time, I am really wearing the gift pants! The third part of the booty that belongs to you as war commander, and which you light heatedly offered to cover the cost of the lost "Vlissingen", came to the tidy sum of 162,500 ducats! That's more than even the precious ""Fantoma"" is worth. In addition there are the recovered 30,000 ducats which captain Opzoom was to deliver to me on the "Vlissingen". You would embarrass me, if you wouldn't regard your flagship as your own. Oh, and here, by the way is the gift certificate."

He walked over to his desk, picked up a ready parchment roll and handed it to his friend. Caprioli took the document and turned it thoughtfully in his hands.

The governor continued:

"The, from the pirates captured brigantines, would have been lost if this Bilg hadn't rescued them.

Therefore, the company does not have a claim on these treasures nor the brigantines; it is satisfied with the recovery of the money from the "Vlissingen" and your payment for the ship and her cargo.

I will inform the gentlemen in Amsterdam accordingly."

Caprioli stroked his goatee with his index finger.

"It appears you want to become a new seaman's saint." he grinned. "However as you do not have the face of a saint, dear Piet, I would like to carefully ask you again what the price for this regal relinquishment is."

"If you are asking about the secret price, you won't even notice when you pay it. So why are you so concerned?"

The governor rubbed his hands together with glee.

"I hope your calculations work out!"

"I'll take you by your word"

He walked to the window and looked down at the harbour.

The long row of ships along the pier was still being admired. A few groups of gesticulating watchers had formed around some of the sailors.

"If you could release the crew rescued off the "Vlissingen" from the service of the company and add a few able seaman, then we could complete the crew of the three brigantines." said Caprioli as if speaking to himself. "We should also be able to find a few good sailors amongst those rescued from the pirates."

The governor approached him.

"For the brigantines you can have them if they are willing. I am sure that the frigates could also spare a few sailors to complete your crews."

"Could you also transfer the gunnery master Bichler to me?"

"With a heavy heart, he is one of our best people; however I can understand that you need a person like him."

Caprioli gripped his friend's arms.

"Piet, I have an idea: would it be possible to have the three brigantines sail under the company's flag, but covering their own expenses?"

The governor thought for a moment.

"If the company will an interest in the business, then yes."

Caprioli lifted his eye brows questioningly.

"And what are these interests...?"

"If for example, a particular count Caprioli should by chance visit St.Petersburg, purely by chance of course, then it would be very nice of him, to mention to the czar that the Holland-West Indies Company would like to purchase all the furs that could be brought to the harbour at a good price. We could ship him precious wood for his palaces, he is still building as if obsessed because he wants to stay on par with the west.

The governor walked back and forth:"only a word you know – but if you say...."

Caprioli's eyes flashed like lightening, embarrassing his friend for a moment

"OK, Piet, if you really want to wait that long, till the wind carries me to St.Petersburg, then I will give the czar the message. But now to reality: the brigantines should belong to Bilg, because he earned them. He should however not be told about this before he attains his captain's licence. Until then, he must think that they belong to the company."

"They can be entered in the register under the name of your *protégé* without him being aware of it. I will get the deeds drawn up today and safe guard them myself."

Caprioli nodded and continued:

"We will form a small company with equal win/loose shares. The brigantines will seemingly be chartered by the company initially, because young Bilg has to get used to being rich first; he doesn't know the dangers yet. As capital, we could use the share of the booty of the sailors that want to come along; the rest of them will get theirs in the hand. After all, the company has decided to forgo their share. What do you think of this idea? To pay off the soldiers is your affair."

"Very, very unusual my dear Cyps, as unusual as everything with you. But if you think..."

Abruptly, after a short pause he asked:

"So, you are sailing to St.Petersburg early tomorrow morning...?"

"You know...?

The governor swayed his head.

"Well yes, I didn't ask you, but we merchants also have our own secret service and above all our secret news gatherers. If we couldn't piece the smallest bits of information together to work out the whole, then we would be very poor merchants. Your actual destination is of no interest to me, but I have a worthwhile load for the brigantines consisting of spices and precious wood. In St.Petersburg they can load furs for Amsterdam. The old crew of the fort will be sent home on board ships I expect here in a few days."

"You should have been a diplomat Piet" said Caprioli laughing.

"I travel better as a merchant, old boy!"

"Oh well, maybe I'll be in St.Petersburg when the ships arrive and maybe I could look after them a bit."

"That would be very good for the new business and the company, Cyps. Tell me, who exactly is this Bilg that played such an important role on your voyage?"

Caprioli shook his shoulders.

"You are asking more than I can answer. I don't even know his real name; he is a very unusual young man. He only wants to be known as Bilg. Larissa told me that the captain of the first ship he served on gave him that name contemptuously. A bilge is the area at the bottom of a ship where all the dirty water collects. A sordid name, but Bilg carries it with distinction. Today, many would be happy to be called Bilg, if they could only be Bilg."

"Do you know why he became a cabin boy?"

"I never asked him that. The destinies of cabin boys are often strange and mysterious. Larissa, which is also strange, befriended him shortly after the start of the voyage. She told me once, that he was searching for his father. An unusual reason to become a cabin boy and a pretty hopeless path.

He seems to come from a good home, judging by his looks and behaviour; not only can he read and write, but also speaks Italian and French. English and Dutch he obviously learned on the ships he served on and German appears to be his native language."

The governor laughed bemused.

"The remarkable thing is, to hear the count Caprioli speak so warmly about a cabin boy!"

"He is a lieutenant after all, my friend!"

"Quite a feat when Caprioli is the commander."

"Exactly, that's why it was a feat; he would have had it easier with someone else."

Caprioli was thoughtful, and quietly he said:" I liked the boy from the beginning, almost like a son."

The gentlemen were quiet and pensive.

The pendulum clock counted the seconds with its Tick Tack, like coins.

Finally the governor asked:

"How is your son by the way, I am his Godfather after all?"

Caprioli sighed.

"I haven't seen him for many years. I had to leave shortly after my wife died. You know yourself how it was during these war times; I couldn't even spend a few weeks at home. I was so happy to be able to spend some time with you, and now...

But I received good news from his teachers and principle."

"And how old are those news..?

"Oh well, probably over two years. It is very difficult not to be travelling when you are in the emperor's secret service."

Again there was silence as they were both deep in thought.

"I would like to know more about this – lieutenant"

The governor interrupted the silence.

"Why? Is he that important to you? You hardly know him."

"As a matter of fact, he is very important to me, Larissa lost her heart to him."

"Larissa..?"

"Why not, he seems to be a good and capable young man and a young lady could easily fall for him."

"That's ridiculous, Piet. Larissa and this – may it be as it will – he is after all a perfect stranger!"

"A moment ago you spoke differently about him..!

"Agreed, but..."

"Never mind 'but '! I can only tell you that if he is what I heard about him, I would welcome him as my son in law. Larissa has money of her own, but she can't buy an honest and upstanding character with that. And Bilg is now such a rich man that Larissa does not have to worry that he would marry her for the sake of her money."

"Bilg would never do that" answered Caprioli more forceful than he intended.

"That's exactly what I wanted to hear from you, Cyps."

"Wise guy!" Said Caprioli snickering. "Your calculations seem to be working out just fine, Piet, even diplomats could learn from you."

The governor winked at him happily.

"The business with Russia is worth far more than relinquishing the booty and the brigantines! And in addition a young man like Bilg as son in law...it seems to me that you still don't follow."

Caprioli looked at his friend with a questioning look.

"Have you forgotten your flying dachshund Witzi? For that I had sworn revenge – I am now taking revenge my way!"

Caprioli laughed.

"And did you forget the barking geese hatching from Witzi's eggs? I also swore revenge for that and I will remember at the right moment!"

The governor suddenly became serious.

"I think that fate is preparing a gratifying surprise for you, that you don't dare to think about."

"What is that supposed to mean, Piet...?

"I don't know exactly yet, but I have assumptions that are close to reality. Give me a bit of time and I will see it clearly."

MORE INTRIGUE FROM SCHEITANOFF

Confused by the sudden change in his fortune, Bilg left the castle and wandered blindly, fleeing from people to the end of this small town. He wanted to be alone with his thoughts. After hours of aimless walking, he wanted to get back to the castle, but found himself in a narrow lane with no idea which way to turn. He didn't see anybody he could ask for directions.

"Well, young man, a bit lost? That can happen to experienced people to!" He heard, coming from a hoarse voice in a dark corner.

Frightened, Bilg took a step backwards. He knew that voice...! From the darkness the short legged form of Scheitanoff slowly appeared.

"Why so afraid, lieutenant Bilg? I am only half as bad as people make me out to be; I could even be a very good friend, if you were a bit friendly with me,"

Bilg backed up more and raised his arms defensively. "Leave me alone, go away, I don't want anything to do with you!" he stammered.

"Not so fast young man" answered Scheitanoff with a secret enticing voice, "You will soon think differently - you are actually expected!"

"Expected....? Where am I expected and by whom?" Bilg answered concerned.

"Over there in the pub!"

Scheitanoff pointed at the dark depth of the gateway with his thumb over his shoulder.

"My friends don't go into dives like that!"

Bilg became angry.

"Don't be so impetuous my young friend, there really is a little person waiting for you in there, that you know really well, a little witch, sweet as can be!" He snapped his fingers with pleasure.

"You lie!" shouted Bilg. "You are a lying rascal!"

Scheitanoff looked at him sadly with his shark eyes.

"You do me an injustice, young man…!"

Bilg abruptly turned away from him.

"Bilg!" he heard someone call at that moment

"Bilg!"

Bilg stared and stopped. That's not possible. Did Larissa's' high voices call him…?

"Well, what did I tell you?"

The wrinkled mouth twisted into a wide grin.

Bilg walked a few quick steps forward and tried to penetrate the darkness with his eyes. A weak hardly noticeable strip of light betrayed a not completely closed door.

He groped a bit further, found a door knob and saw that he was standing on the threshold of a harbour pub. The saloon was almost empty. A fat waiter was dosing at the bar. A half drunk sailor sat in one corner, with a glass of rum, staring at nothing and strumming a wistful melody on his guitar.

"Bilg!" he heard a low almost whispering voice. His eyes followed the sound.

At a table, in the darkest corner, he thought he recognised a figure by the flickering oil lamp. A stuffed crocodile hung from the smoke covered ceiling above her. With a beating heart he approached the table – and stood before Larissa!

"My God what are you doing here? How did you get here..? He stammered.

The girl smiled.

"I was waiting for you, because I absolutely have to speak to you alone!"

She moved over and Bilg sat down mesmerised.

"But how could you know that I would be here? I got lost!"

He looked at her beautiful shimmering teeth.

"The yearning, Bilg – I am a woman... and beside that Paramaribo is my home."

The waiter, curious, came waddling over to ask what he wanted. He pointed at the rather large tin mug standing in front of Larissa. The waiter also brought him a mug of 'Malvasier' and disappeared behind his bottles at the bar.

"Well Bilg, isn't this a wonderfully secret and quiet spot for words that only concern us?" Larissa continued.

Bilg had still not recovered and stared into his mug. During the whole voyage, he ever only saw Larissa with one glass of wine and even that one she only sipped at like a bird.

He took a tiny sip. The heavy wine went like a fire storm through his body.

"Don't you like me anymore, Bilg?" he heard Larissa saying.

He looked at her.

"Why do you ask...?"

Yes those were Larissa's' beautiful black eyes – but they didn't have the sheen that he became to love so much on the ship.

"Well..." she insisted.

"On the ship you knew it and didn't have to ask me!" he answered with quivering lips.

She gently placed her hand on his – for the first time.

"I have to be completely sure now, vida mia, amor mia – my life, my love – completely sure, before I ask my father." She breathed.

He had never heard her speak Spanish, except with Borromaus.

"What do you want to ask him...?"

"Oh, if he will let us get married, muy amor mio!"

He wanted to pull his hand away, but couldn't.

"Not now, Bilg – but in a few years – but I have to know if I can wait for you", she continued in a whisper.

He stared at her hand, something was strange about it.

"Where is that beautiful ring you always wore on the ""Fantoma"" and never took off?" he asked.

"Oh, that one....? I had it taken to the goldsmith, the stone needed polishing."

Why did he never notice that Larissa had such hands: long, pointed and crooked fingers, with nails that almost looked like claws; they reminded him of spider legs.

Larissa slid so close to him that he could feel the heat of her arm.

"Can I tell my father...?" she returned tenderly to her question.

Bilg pouted in defiance.

"First I have to find my father!"

Larissa laughed loudly.

"You're looking for your father; and yet he was on board the "Fantoma" for the entire long voyage – you spoke with him uncountable times!"

Aghast he looked at the girl next to him. She moved closer to him. He couldn't evade her.

"Do you know who uncle Cyps actually is...?" she crooned.

"Count Caprioli? Your godfather but ..."

"Yes, but what is his real name?"

In Bilg's' head the world started to turn.

"Does he have another name...?

"Yes, the same as yours!"

Bilg lent away from her.

"Leave my father out of this, Larissa!"

His throat and lips were dry from anger and confusion.

Larissa smiled with a mischievous look in her eyes.

"His name is Cyprian Amadeus Count Fantoroso, and you were born on his estates."

"Larissa, if that's true, how come you didn't tell me on the ship?"

"Could you prove without papers that you are a count Fantoroso? Du you really think, that uncle Cyps would have recognised his missing son, in a slippery cabin boy?"

"But I became a lieutenant without papers, Larissa."

She laughed.

"Yes, because I explained everything to my father before, otherwise, uncle Cyps could never have bought the officer's certificate from him."

"And what proof do you have...?

"More than enough, Bilg: your nature, your special awareness, your usual caution and bravery. When count Caprioli trusted you with the command of the "Fantoma", you accepted it so naturally – but above all, your knowledge of the Fantoroso castle and the family. We spoke about it often enough."

Bilg's' head sank and his hands shook. He closed his eyes, unable to utter another word. Dark dream shadows surrounded him. His thoughts formed images - happy ones, terrifying, unreal images that swirled and danced around him.

When after some time he looked up again, rubbed his eyes - he was alone.

Frightened he jumped up.

"Waiter...!"

The fat waiter shuffled over.

"Your order lieutenant...?"

"Where is the lady that I was talking to?"

"The lady? She left a long time ago, Sir." wondered the waiter. "You fell asleep and I didn't want to disturb you. Your one of the crew of the "Fantoma" are you not?"

Bilg rubbed his head. "I fell asleep...?"

The waiter knew not to show surprise at the unusual behaviour of his guest.

"Well, why shouldn't you have nodded off? I am sure you must be very tired from the efforts of your long voyage – one hears so much about the adventures of the "Fantoma"."

Bilg looked into the mugs in front of him: Larissa's' was empty, his own almost untouched.

"Can you give me directions back to the castle, waiter?"

"I'll send a servant to show you the way lieutenant; you wouldn't find it on your own"

He answered officiously.

"What time is it?"

"Oh, by the time you get there the sun will almost be up."

Bilg threw a coin on the table.

"Call the servant waiter; I have to get to the castle quickly."

The fat one shuffled away in servitude.

The servant, whose back was bent from the burden of his years, guided him through the dirty streets.

"One says that your count is a magician, Sir" He said, trying to start a conversation.

"Nonsense...!" protested Bilg.

But the old one didn't let go:

"The young lady who spoke with you, is she also part of his party? I saw her – she is not from here.

Sutler maybe or something like that...?"

The dry voice of the old one sounded, as if it came from far away – as if the wind carried it to his ears in loud and then low wisps. Bilg didn't pay attention – his thoughts were with Larissa.

"It was the governors' daughter" he said, without really knowing whether he answered a question or not.

The old one chuckled mockingly and mischievously.

Bilg tried to recognise the dark form of the servant – terrified he stopped in his tracks. Scheitanoff..?

But it was too dark to see any more than the sharp outlines of the man next to him.

A cool gust of wind almost blew off his hat – sand crunched lightly under his feet.

The undulating line of the beach shimmered behind the last house.

The servant stopped and raised his arm:"there...! He said.

A sneering chuckle followed that word.

"Was it really Scheitanoff...?"

Bilg's' eyes searched the emptiness.

The servant was gone – as if the wind had blown him away.

About two miles away, high above the town, he saw the festive and inviting shimmering of the castle windows.

Bilg got under way.

DISAPPEARED!

A clear star studded night descended over the town and castle of Paramaribo. The first guest carriages rolled up the wide road to the castle. Liveried valets stood by with their storm lanterns to receive the festively dressed ladies and gentlemen. The inhabitants of the castle were however, in a barely disguised state of unrest: since that afternoon the young lieutenant Bilg, about whom the whole town was talking, had disappeared without a trace. Larissa, who with her father had the job of greeting the guests, was constantly thinking about her friend, could barely keep her countenance.

Caprioli was having a chat with the ship and castle officers while waiting in the reception hall. They were all dressed in their finest dress uniforms, except Borromaus, the gunnery officer, who could not part from his pirates' costume. With a mocking twinkle in his eye he examined the finery of the ladies and gentlemen, pulled up his trousers, tightened his belt a notch and growled:

"Bah, what's good for life and death at sea, is three times better than these groomed land lubbers!"

Caprioli left him with his opinion and kept quiet as Borromaus walked around Captain Bull eye -balling him with his feathered hat, bright red sash, prancing like a fattened turkey with a peacock tail.

By and by the guests streamed in, passing the group in shy admiration, pointing out the count in whispers. Caprioli, a head taller than the rest, stood out with his nonchalant smile and quiet elegance. Pelegrin and especially Habakuk standing next to the count were also duly admired. The stories told by the sailors and soldiers, by now heavily embroidered, had spread from the kitchens, to the servants quarters and from there to rooms of the guests and finally to every house in the town.

It took another half hour before the rest of the guests arrived.

The governor entered the dining hall with Larissa, greeted the assembly and introduced the adventurous seamen.

As much as Pieter van Groenhagen tried to show a cheerful front, he was angry that his big surprise for the evening wasn't happening. His suspicion was confirmed when the scribe brought him the officer's certificate to sign and when he saw the young lieutenants' name: He was Caprioli's' son! If Larissa suspected it or had actually been told by Bilg himself, he didn't know.

Servants walked amongst the guests with appetite inspiring liqueurs and offered them in sparkling glasses.

Greetings between acquaintances, discussions and exchanges of news went on throughout the large hall. A group of inquisitive people had soon gathered around the officers, wanting to know more than the taciturn seaman and soldiers could tell them. Borromaus escaped angrily, stomping through the hall on his wooden leg, to a large window where he hid behind a curtain looking down to the harbour at the ships. Their silhouettes and lights were easily distinguished against the dark night sky.

The governor took Caprioli aside.

"What do you think about Bilg...?" he asked with concern.

"An incomprehensible insubordination" answered the count with a voice in which disappointment, worry and strength competed.

"I don't believe that Cyps – an accident perhaps...?"

"Assumptions are useless, old friend, we can only send out a search party for him and wait. By the way, since we landed, Bilg is under your command, so it's up to you to judge him. Too bad about the young one, he could have gone far!"

The governor silently looked at his friend and turned to his other guests.

Caprioli smiled after him and twirled his monocle on its fine gold chain around his finger. Of course, he too was concerned about Bilg, but an unmistakable feeling told him that the boy was alright. Maybe one of the pretty young ladies of this strange land tempted him, maybe he was invited and the wine was too much for him, maybe... Assumptions! Caprioli was angry at himself.

What was important at the moment, that the governor had betrayed himself: his unrest proved that Bilg was just as important to him.

He strolled towards the castle commander, who in his gold bristling uniform, was in the process of explaining to a swarm of ladies surrounding him, what would have happened if the giant sea snake, didn't have such a special appetite for cannon balls and empty barrels.

The ladies, with pale faces and staring eyes held their hands over their mouths.

"You are here count…?"

Caprioli felt a slight touch on his elbow. He turned around and found himself looking at Scheitanoff.

"That's perfect!"Said the fat little dawdler with a hypocritical laugh "from what I hear your s… I mean, lieutenant Fa…, I meant to say Bilg: disappeared and is being searched for."

"You're all I needed, Scheitanoff!" His eyes like lightning bolts. "Since when do you stutter…?

"Ha, ha – the liquor is burning my throat a bit."

"It's burning you…? Caprioli had to laugh spontaneously.

"What business do you have with Bilg? Have you got your dirty hands in this…?

Scheitanoff raised his hands in defence.

"I…? How can you think that, Count, when I am always so concerned! I might be able to give you a hint though; you know that I have many connections."

"I have no interest in your hints or connections! I am not interested in a dead lieutenant Bilg."

"Who is talking about a dead Bilg?"

Scheitanoff almost screeched.

Caprioli looked at him sideways.

"So, you do have your dirty hands in this affair and Bilg is alive. That's all I wanted to know!"

The infernal Excellency bit his lips. As if Bilg had never been mentioned he asked with undisguised viciousness:

"What if I were to introduce you to the assembly by your real name, count...?"

Blue lightening shot from narrowed eyes. Caprioli twirled the end of his goatee.

"A little blackmail this time?"

"One does what one can, count."

"Whatever you like, it won't hurt me and it won't help you. In return I will inform the assembly of your real reason for your diplomatic mission here – I am afraid however, that you will hardly be able to increase your clientele here."

"Well parried!" heckled Scheitanoff hoarsely."

Caprioli coughed.

"Listen carefully Scheitanoff" The count emphasized *every* word, "Of course you know that I am leaving tomorrow morning. Your more or less bad jokes always amused me on the voyages, no doubt without them I would have been bored quite often. I suggest, let's say an agreement ,only because I would like some peace from you: within five minutes, due to one of my jokes you will disappear from this hall and these surroundings and let yourself cool down for three months and spare me your presence. Should I not succeed...?"

"Ha, Ha, Ha!" Scheitanoff's insolent laughter interrupted him, "You don't have to add anything, and the joke is too good! Within five minutes you say? Ha, ha, ho, ho – agreed: you will do nothing to prevent my disappearance for five minutes!"

At that moment, the sister of the archbishop, Dona Escamalota swished by.

"A word, gracious baroness!" Caprioli stopped her with a charming smile. Happy to be addressed by the famous count, she stopped. Caprioli reverently kissed her hand. "May I introduce the infernal representative, his Excellency Natas Scheitanoff?"

The baroness looked at the deformed figure, let her eyes glide over the round head with the wrinkled skin and shark eyes, and with a sour sweet smile, extended her hand to Scheitanoff.

"An uncomfortable name!" she whispered to Caprioli, "where is his land situated...?"

"Oh, somewhere down there, it is very hot there", answered Caprioli, playing with his monocle.

"I thought so, - unattractive people, you agree, count?" she added whispering.

Scheitanoff, suddenly chocked in a spasmodic cough, pressed a handkerchief to his mouth, and gasped fighting for air.

"What is wrong with him suddenly...? The baroness asked perplexed with her pointy lips, her thin eye brows pulled up like church windows.

"His Excellency must have inhaled something unpleasant", Caprioli answered with a smirk.

Scheitanoff had bent over the hand of the baroness, and the lingering smell of incense, must have entered his sensitive nose.

"Puff" and the infernal representative was gone.

"Madonna, how about that!" said the baroness disgusted. She coughed slightly, and held her crochet handkerchief to her nose. She wasn't frightened; sudden disappearances like this didn't seem uncommon to her.

"That is the custom down there", explained Caprioli, "but I still allowed myself to introduce his Excellency, as it is always useful to remember a face like that."

"Anyway, he wouldn't be received in my home!"

"He would hardly dare to announce himself to you, dear baroness."

"I hope this was the only impolite and foul smelling member amongst your acquaintances, count!" she answered sharply.

"Hasta la vista! - Good bye!"

"Hasta luego, baroness!" Caprioli bowed deeply.

She floated away, carefully avoiding mixing her holy perfume with Scheitanoff's invisible legacy. Caprioli rubbed his chin and looked after her, and then he slowly walked over to his companions.

FAREWELL

The servant opened the double doors to a resplendent hall, glimmering with candlelight. In the middle of the large room stood the dinner table adorned with flowers.

The head steward ceremoniously tapped his staff three times.

"Take your places, ladies and gentlemen!" called the governor, offered his arm to Dona Escamalota and escorted her to the head of the table on his right. Larissa sat to the left of the governor, and Caprioli beside her. The rest of the laughing and chatting guests were shown their places, according to dignity and rank, by the stewards.

Time passed quickly with feasting, toasts and speeches. However, it would be rare, at a feast like this, to see so little consumed; all eyes kept wondering to Caprioli, to the pretty Larissa and the unusual companions of the count. Hundreds of ears, tried to catch the smallest word coming from their lips.

Borromaus, looked at his plate without interruption, and silently consumed one chicken leg after the other.

Nieselpriem's nose shone more than normal, and he regularly had to wipe a droplet with the back of his hand, so it wouldn't fall in his plate. With every bite, Captain Bull peered at the huge, floor to ceiling mirrors; he couldn't get enough of looking at his resplendent image. These mirrors covered every wall making the hall look gigantic, and transformed the candlelight of the chandeliers into a flood of light. Pelegrin, picked at his plate, like old men do, and ate little. Habakuk, to the contrary, only had eyes for fried and backed delicacies, which he had to do without for so long, and had his plate refilled again and again by the waiters.

Caprioli watched him with amusement; but got goose bumps every time the moor shovelled down another portion.

Every once in a while, the name Bilg was whispered in astonishment, behind covered mouths. But, no one dared to ask the governor or the count about the cabin boy, who, for bravery had been promoted to lieutenant, and those who worried about him, deliberately paid attention to his whispered name. Only when someone passed the information around the table that, the lieutenant as the youngest officer on the "Fantoma", had to take over the watch, did they stopped asking about him.

After the last toast, the governor stood up terminating the dinner. A swarm of servants rolled the heavy tables out, and rearranged the chairs in a semicircle around seafarers. Baked sweets and liqueurs were served on small tables, and offered to the guests after their heavy meal. Finally, they all hoped, they would hear, from Caprioli's mouth and that of his officers, what was behind the fantastic stories that had gone from mouth to mouth, since the arrival of the fleet. But the men remained silent. Even Caprioli, whom the governor himself had asked for a report, shook his head smiling. He was well known as skilled narrator of funny stories, but it wasn't his style to give himself airs with his own adventures. So, Larissa had to entertain the guests by giving them a report of the adventures on this long journey. Although her heart was heavy for Bilg, the more she told, the more enthusiastic she became. Soon all eyes looked at her lips spellbound. Sounds of astonishment and every once in a while, roaring laughter when she recounted the story of a frightening adventure, which ended in an unexpected and surprising result.

Captain Bull, sweating, slid back and forth on his chair, and tortured his brain in vain, trying to find a chance to escape from the present company.

But Larissa didn't say anything that could hurt him or make him smile. When he gave her a beseeching look at dangerous parts of her story, she just smiled and found a more sparing way to tell it. Nieselpriem and Borromaus were not happy about the report because of that; they would have preferred to drown the captain in a shower of laughter. But because Caprioli said nothing, they didn't dare to interrupt Larissa. However when she wanted to omit telling about her sabre fight with the pirate captain, the gunnery chief couldn't hold back any more.

"Caramba, senora mia!" he started, "that goes too far!"

And then he started, in his growling and chopped up way of speaking, to tell how Larissa, with whistling foil strokes averted the attack of the heavy sabre, cornered the character and then with one stab of her foil through his piled up hair, had nailed him to the mast.

The guests had listened breathless and rewarded the fabulous and Borromaus' tale with loud and prolonged applause.

The guests barely noticed when an officer approached the governor, and whispered to him and Caprioli, that the "Fantoma" was ready for sea, and the crews part of the loot, stored under guard in the commander's cabin. Caprioli thanked the officer and quietly passed the news on to Bull, Borromaus and Nieselpriem. The three, breathed a sigh of relief. They found their position very unpleasant.

When Larissa, in her droll way, also told them of the adventure with the sea snake, and the secret of how the fleet, without wind and stowed sails had rushed across the ocean and in to the harbour, was revealed, Caprioli got up. But he had to wait with his address, till the guests, exhausted from laughing, could breathe normally again. Erect, to his full height, the left hand on the pommel of his sabre, the count tapped his glass.

"Ladies and gentlemen!

On behalf of all my companions on this journey, of which, coming from a lovely and educated mouth, we just heard a witty description, I thank you, his Excellency Pieter van Groenhagen, the assembled guests, and the whole population of Paramaribo, for the festive reception that was prepared for us."

He bent down to his friend and whispered a few words to him.

The governor waved the head steward over and gave him some instructions.

"I would have liked to grant the crew of the "Fantoma" a few restful days in Paramaribo", Caprioli continued. "As everyone knows, I only took on the duties of commanding the fleet, to see my old friend, his

Excellency the governor, again, and to spend a few restful days hunting with him. Things changed. On my arrival, the order to start a new journey the next morning was waiting for me. The "Fantoma" is ready for sea, and we depart in half an hour on our new voyage."

For a few seconds, the happy listeners sat as if paralysed, than the storm of protests started. The guests jumped up and beseeched the count to stay a few more days, or at least only a single day.

Caprioli, smiling lifted his hand asking to be allowed to continue.

He made an imposing figure, in his gold stitched midnight blue tailcoat and sparkling medal.

"An order, ladies and gentlemen, knows no restrictions, especially in these war torn times", he continued. "All of us find parting difficult, and pointless protests make it even bitterer. If things would have gone as planned, I would have requested a special celebration in the next few days: we captured the three brigantines that are lying in the harbour from the pirates. They will be sailing under the Dutch-West Indies company flag but have terrible names. As we don't have enough time to rebaptise them now, the governor will invite his eminence the arch bishop and the whole population of this hospitable town, in the next few days, to a baptism feast. But now, we want to find names for these ships, and drink to their future successful voyages. I suggest, that the most eloquent among us, Senorita Larissa van Groenhagen, decides the first name."

"Bilg!" shouted Larissa. She jumped up from her seat and again called:"Bilg should be the name of the first brigantine, yes uncle Cyps?"

The waiters were handing tall slim glasses, filled with a white gold sparkling wine to the guests.

Caprioli, smiling, lifted his glass.

The guests, delighted by the count's idea jumped up.

"Bilg shall be the name of the first brigantine!" shouted Caprioli. "Sadly, the young officer, who gave this name so much meaning, is not among us, but I think he will be present at the baptism festivities."

Before the guests had time to ask about Bilg's where about, the count continued:

"Because, lieutenant Bilg and Senorita Larissa not only shared the many dangers of the journey, but also saved the already captured brigantines from sinking, I suggest to baptise the second brigantine with the name Larissa!"

Cheering, the guests agreed. With a look and a silent bow, the governor thanked his friend for honouring his daughter. But his thoughts immediately strayed. His eyes kept searching the door to the banquet hall.

Larissa herself, stood there with a bright red face, and was barely able to curtsey to say thank you.

"And now, ladies and gentlemen, it is time to find a name for the third brigantine", reminded Caprioli.

In the moment of silence that followed, Larissa took a step forward, looked at her god father with beaming eyes and turned to the assembly.

"Honoured guests, I think the third brigantine, can only carry one name, the one we are all thinking about. She shall be called "Caprioli" and be the flag ship of this little fleet!"

A new storm of cheers broke out, and only died down when the governor himself asked for a word. As if he wanted to gain time, he approached the old captain Opzoom with a deep breath, guided him to the front of the semi circle and explained:"Mijnheer Opzoom, one of our best captains, through none of his fault, lost his ship the "Vlissingen to pirates. My friend Caprioli with his brave companions managed to save the majority of the crew and return them safely to Paramaribo. Furthermore, they saved the gold that the "Vlissingen" was to bring to us. In addition, count Caprioli donated his part of the prise money to the company; with that, the ship and its cargo are paid for. If my friend Caprioli agrees with me, we cannot find a better and more deserving person, a person so badly affected by bad luck, than Dierk Opzoom, as captain of the "Caprioli" and also commander of the little fleet.

"Hurrah, Hurrah, hurrah, commodore Opzoom!"

The guests agreed with loud cheers, raised their glasses and drank to the old sea bear.

Caprioli was the first one to congratulate him and welcome him as commodore.

Confused, with teary eyes the white bearded man stammered his thanks.

Caprioli pushed him down on his chair, waived to his companions and continued:

"Farewells, ladies and gentlemen, should be quick, as quick as the wind. I ask for your permission to say goodbye now and to let me and my companions return to the "Fantoma" unescorted. The majority of the officers who shared our adventures are staying here, and will no doubt continue to enjoy the festivities in the company of this esteemed assembly. I, however promise: Should a complete calm fill our stowed sails again and bring us to this vicinity – it doesn't necessarily have to involve a sea snake - , then we will not forget our new friends. Good bye!"

He shook hands with his friend the governor once more.

Larissa, jumped on a chair, wrapped her arms around Caprioli's neck and kissed both his cheeks.

"Tell me, uncle Cyps, what is happening with Bilg?" she whispered in his ear.

"Don't worry; I have the feeling that you will have him, unharmed, soon again. Scheitanoff probably played a trick on him."

"Scheitanoff...?" frightened, she asked.

"Yes, he was here earlier and then suddenly disappeared."

"This wretched scoundrel!"

Caprioli gently moved her arms from his neck.

"Will you really go to sea without Bilg, uncle Cyps?"

"I can't wait any longer Larissa, but be happy that you can keep him with you a bit longer. Scheitanoff can't hurt him physically!"

"I will follow you, uncle Cyps – with him!"

She jumped off the chair and held on to his arm.

Caprioli bowed to the guests, waived to them and with his officers, walked to the exit of the hall.

"Uncle Cyps...!" whispered Larissa.

"Yes my dear...?"

"My Baba is on board the "Fantoma", secretly you know – because of Habakuk, but he doesn't know. She wants to marry him. Is she allowed?"

"Nice things you do behind my back – but OK, she will be very useful!"

He embraced Larissa and whispered in her ear:

"Now I can tell you – I also did something behind your back: In a separate section of the stables, you will find Sala – she will soon be giving birth. Sala is yours!"

"Oh, uncle Cyps...!"

Larissa was beside herself with happiness.

"Ladies and gentlemen", the governor now addressed the assembly, "I will accompany the count to the castle gates – my daughter will represent me in the meanwhile."

Quickly, he followed his friend and held his arm.

Silently, the high double doors closed behind them, the officers, Pelegrin and Habakuk.

In the ante rooms, Pieter van Groenhagen, held Caprioli back:

"Cyps, I have to tell you something – I waited to the last moment with that. It was to have been the big surprise of the evening – and at the same time, my delayed revenge for your goose dachshund Witzi."

Caprioli stopped and with raised eye brows looked at his friend.

My mood for jokes has passed for the evening, Piet – because of Bilg."

"This concerns Bilg – I know his real name!"

"Is that important now...?"

"Yes Cyps – Bilg is Maximilian Count Fantoroso...I have undeniable proof!"

Caprioli froze. He pressed his lips together. Seconds later he said:

"Should he re appear, you will test him. If it's not his fault, then give him my regards – he can reach me in St.Petersburg. Should I miss him there, he can go to the secret cabinet in Vienna, to find out where I am; I will ask baron Hojos to give him the information."

"Is that all...?

"Everything Piet – because at this moment and under these circumstances nothing else could happen!"

Caprioli, shook his friend's hand once more, turned and quickly followed his officers.

NEAR THE GOAL

Even when the governor returned, it took quite some time before the guests recovered from the shock of Caprioli's and his officer's sudden departure. Gloomy conversations drifted through the hall. The relaxed mood only returned, when Larissa bravely, told Caprioli's story of the goose dachshund Witzi, and jokingly teased her father with it. The governor, used to be master of his feelings, but enticed by the happiness around him, started to tell stories himself, stories he had experienced with Caprioli, many years ago.

About an hour had passed, when the joyful entertainment was suddenly interrupted by the head steward.

Dignified, he tapped the floor three times with his staff. The double doors opened wide.

"Lieutenant Maximilian count Fantoroso!" He announced with a distinct voice.

Bilg stood in the door frame.

For seconds, even the smallest sound froze on the lips.

Aghast, Larissa stared at Bilg. She took a small step towards him.

Bilg saluted the governor and bowed to the assembly.

His Excellency, van Groenhagen slowly stood up, guided Bilg into the hall and introduced him to the surprised guests, as the awaited lieutenant, who during the journey, rose from cabin boy to lieutenant.

Count Fantoroso...? Wasn't this lieutenant called Bilg till now...?

Bilg still felt trapped in a wild dream. He discovered Larissa, forgot everything around him and asked with quivering lips:

"How did you end up in that squalid den of thieves...?

Laboriously, the words were wrestled from his lips.

"What are you talking about? In which den of thieves was I supposed to have been...?

I don't go into dives!"

Confusion, worry about Bilg and indignation all in one were painted on her face.

He took her hand. "You are wearing the ring; it is really your hand! He stuttered. He looked at her. Yes, and those are your eyes again!"

The governor forced him to sit and put a glass in his hand. He gulped down the wine.

Not one of the guests dared to say a word.

"What happened to you, where were you lieutenant? We had to wait a long time for you!"

The governor's voice was low and severe, trying to get Bilg back to normal.

Bilg jumped up and mumbled an apology. He didn't notice that he held on to Larissa hand. The governor saw it and smiled unnoticeable.

"You got lost and thought you discovered Larissa in a harbour side pub...? He said mockingly.

He wanted to provoke Bilg's resistance.

Only now, the tension imprisoning Bilg eased. The words flowed like a river over his lips, when he recounted his adventures with Scheitanoff and Larissa look alike. He didn't mention that the false Larissa claimed that he was Caprioli's son; the thought alone was outrageous.

"Who is Scheitanoff...?" one of the guests asked cautiously.

The infernal excellence had not been mentioned by anyone till now. As if by agreement, everyone who talked about the adventures of the trip concealed any experiences with him.

Now, Larissa told the disbelieving assembly what she knew about Scheitanoff, and how he continuously tried to bring misfortune to the sailors, soldiers and ships.

If I didn't know how level headed you are, and if it wasn't you telling this story, Larissa, I would have to believe that I was listening to fairy tales. A few hours ago I saw this character myself, count Caprioli introduced him to me", interrupted Dona Escamalota.

"He was here, in this hall and the count introduced him to you...? Pieter van Groenhagen didn't understand anything anymore.

The assembly dispersed into small excited discussion groups.

To get some clarity, the governor led his daughter and the young lieutenant to a quiet window sill. But before he could say what depressed him so much, Bilg started to report. He explained that he only let himself be delayed so long, because the false Larissa claimed that he was count Caprioli's son, and that she had self evident reasons for her claim. When Bilg finished, Larissa said:

"Then you really are uncle Cyps' son! I thought so, I knew it when you showed me your sleeping corner on the "Fantoma" and I let you look at my medallion!"

"What are you saying...?"Bilg went pale. "I am really supposed to be count Caprioli's son? Then the false Larissa in the pub didn't lie...?"

The governor cleared his throat and said thoughtfully:

"No, this phantom did not lie, but did something far worse:"You let yourself be taken in by this Scheitanoff, although you recognised him, and lost many precious hours."

Bilg too agitated to understand the meaning of the governor's words, asked:

"And what makes you so sure that I am the count's son...?"

"I was only sure when I read your name on the officers certificate - , it is the real family name of my friend Caprioli, and beside him, you are the only one that carries that name. Only very few know this and those few keep it to themselves. You must have guessed that yourself, else why did you not say anything in front of the assembly?"

"I didn't want people to think that I am boasting!" In his excitement, he answered in a manner not becoming his rank. "Couldn't I have falsified the name, Excellency? I had no papers, and your notary had to take my word for it, as I was forced to admit to my name."

"I have told my daughter too much about you, lieutenant, mostly things that we were very familiar with and that could have only been known by you. Your personality fits those things. Besides that, you have a birth mark on your left shoulder..."

"Nobody could know that!" Bilg exclaimed.

The governor smiled:"no, none of us – but Pelegrin knew about it; he knew you when you were a little boy.

I secretly discussed this with him, dear god son. He suspected it for a long time, but the birth mark alone wasn't enough. That is why he kept quiet."

Bilg had missed that the governor suddenly spoke to him in a familiar tone, but Larissa noticed it. Happily she put her hand on her father's arm and squeezed it thankfully.

"And where is my..., where is count Caprioli now? Where are the "Fantoma" and her crew...? Said Bilg highly agitated.

The governor placed his hands on Bilg's shoulders: "on his arrival in Paramaribo, an order to immediately start a new journey awaited him – you arrived too late for the farewell dinner. He and his officers left us a bit more than an hour ago."

"And you told him nothing about me...?"

Bilg was outside of himself.

The governor dabbed his chin with a silk handkerchief.

"I told him everything!"

"And he still didn't wait for me...?"

The governor answered seriously: "When an order affects the voluntarily taken responsibility, then feelings have to be silenced – were it any other way, no ship could sail and no country could be governed. Your father wouldn't be Caprioli, if he sacrificed his feelings for his duty. But he sends his greetings and initially he expects you in St.Petersburg."

At his signal, the servants pulled back the heavy curtains on the front wall of the hall, and opened the doors leading to the terrace.

Bright daylight flooded the hall.

The governor turned to his guests: "Ladies and gentlemen, with luck, we may still see the "Fantoma" - the terrace gives you an uninterrupted view."

With one arm around Larissa shoulder and the other around Bilg's, they walked out into the open.

The guests pressed out behind them.

The sails of the "Fantoma" shone far out in the ocean. Bilg, not able to utter a word, stood frozen gazing into the distance.

"We will follow your father – soon!" Larissa tried to console him. He didn't hear it.

Caprioli must have seen the assembly with his spyglass.

The muzzle flash of her cannons could be seen on the "Fantoma".

Seconds later, the windows in Paramaribo, vibrated from the farewell salute.

Bilg walked up to the balustrades and waved both his arms.

The governor handed him a spyglass; He and Larissa looked at the ship the same way.

Something surprising happened at that moment: a stream of fire, brighter than the sun, seemed to tear the "Fantoma" apart, a mountain of black smoke rolled across the ocean.

With a salvo from its eighty cannons, the "Fantoma" said that the young lieutenant had been recognised.

A second salvo followed – and a third.

The houses of Paramaribo shook.

Bilg cried out in jubilation: "Bilg, look...!"

The spyglass pressed to his eye, Bilg saw at the top of the foremast, the raising of a burgee and stop directly under Caprioli's.

Both bore the same emblem...

www.ingramcontent.com/pod-product-compliance
Lightning Source LLC
Chambersburg PA
CBHW061344310726
48974CB00001B/191